Puckerbrush
Milestones on the Journey to Manhood

Bob McCrillis

Puckerbrush

Milestones on the Journey to Manhood

Bob McCrillis

W C P

Pearl S. Buck Writing Center Press

DEDICATION

To Mrs. Helen Hutchins. I don't think either of us realized how critical a turning point it was. Thank you.

Contents

ACKNOWLEDGMENTS

Without my wife, Linda's patience and support, this would have become another boldly-begun and readily-abandoned effort in my file cabinet.. The stories wouldn't have been worth reading if it were not for the encouragement and guidance provided by Dr. Anne K. Kaler. Our sessions often resembled two Irishmen arguing in a pub, but the stories were the better for it. The support from the Pearl S. Buck Writers Guild was also critical in keeping me moving in the right direction.

Awareness

The Doe

"George, he's just too young," my mother snapped. "It's bad enough that you allow him to hang around with the men, but twelve is too young to hunt with a big rifle."

"He's plenty old enough…"

She cut him off, "You just want to show him off. What happens if he gets hurt? He's just too young."

"Get dressed, Patrick," he said to me. "We're going hunting."

The Old Man's spare red-plaid coat and pants were scratchy and hard to walk in and his red hat kept falling in front of my eyes but I was beaming when I got back to the kitchen. My mother stood at the sink with her back to us. She was scrubbing a pot as if she wanted to take the enamel off. She didn't say a word when we left.

The snow-covered roads were a bit of a challenge but we slid into camp about two in the afternoon. Judging from the cars, Danny, Charlie and my uncles were already there along with others whose trucks I didn't recognize. At least there'd be a fire built already and we wouldn't have to wait a half hour before we took our coats off.

We clumped through the door, stomping the snow off our boots to a chorus of "where the hell have you been, George?"

Everyone in the room knew that the Old Man worked Saturday mornings, but they teased him anyway.

Someone yelled, "And I see you brought the marksman with you." The praise didn't fool me – I was just a kid with a little rifle – but I lapped it up anyway. It gave me an identity in the group. If the weather wasn't too bad, the men might even challenge each other to shooting competitions with my .22. Of course, the beer consumption assured that I was the only one who could hit anything.

The Old Man sent me back up to the car to get the stuff out of the back and the rifles. The stuff consisted of half a dozen huge cans of beef stew, three dozen eggs, bacon and Wonder Bread. Oh, and two cases of Pabst Blue Ribbon beer.

The poker game had already begun. From what I could see through the haze of cigarette smoke, my Uncle John was the early winner. I set the food and the beer on the floor in the corner away from the woodstove – didn't want the beer to get warm – and looked over to the Old Man.

"You ready to go, Patrick?" he asked. When I nodded that I was, he heaved his coat back on and steered me toward the door by my shoulder. He grabbed his deer rifle from the rack as we got to the door.

"Now we know why you bothered to bring the rifle, George," Danny laughed, "you're going to let the marksman get you a deer."

Uncle John chimed in, "Better watch out, Patrick, that rifle hasn't been fired in ten years – probably still got the cartridges your father got when he bought the damn gun." It was a running joke that most of the men came on these hunting and fishing trips to get away from the wives, drink beer and play cards.

The Doe

"You know, Paddy," Uncle Connor said, "one year your father left that .30-30 in the back of my truck for the whole season – never even missed it."

"Yeah, Connor, but I took plenty of money off you, didn't I?" Then he turned to me, "Never mind those jokers, Boy. Let's get you set up to get a deer." And he shoved me out the door.

We walked down an old logging track that turned off the camp road. I watched for deer sign in the thin snow and reveled in my adventure. After a mile or so, he handed me the rifle. Then he dug into his pocket and brought out what I thought of as the *sacred cartridges*. The very ones Uncle John claimed were older than I was. Whether they had actually reached the mythical age my uncles claimed, the shells were certainly old. They were decorated with green streaks of corrosion on the brass and black goop on the copper jackets. They looked like talismans of some ancient ritual. Since he never left the camp, he never loaded or fired his rifle so the cartridges lived on year after year. I hoped they would still fire.

"Load the rifle, but don't put one in the chamber yet." He led me off the track and through the trees and heavy brush to a muddy little trickle that ran roughly parallel with the trail. He pointed to an opening in the dense brush on the other side of the stream. "That's where they'll come out, if they're around. See the hoof prints?" He turned back to me. "Got your whistle?" I nodded. "Good, use it if you need to move around. You don't want some jerk to think you're a deer. I'll pick you up before it gets dark." He started back toward the logging trail. He turned and yelled, "I'll signal with my whistle when I get close so don't shoot me."

Well, here I was, just me and my rifle – Daniel Boone junior.

The stiff late-November wind was making my ears and nose sting and my eyes water. I needed to be downwind but sheltered if I wasn't going to freeze solid before any deer showed up. A little ways downstream the ripped up roots of a downed maple made an

5

eight-foot-high mound and a crater I could hide in. I'd be protected from the wind and still have a clear shot at any deer crossing the stream. The crater wasn't even very muddy.

Before settling in, I worked the lever of the old .30-30 to load a round into the rifle's chamber and lowered the hammer to the half cock safe position. Nothing to do now but to wait.

An hour went by, then another. The watery sunlight faded into twilight, and near darkness under the trees. The moan of the wind in the trees and the gurgle of the stream combined with the warm envelope created by my oversize wool jacket put me in a kind of trance. I sat with unfocused eyes, snug and dreamy becoming another lump in the landscape. The cold and change of the light didn't matter to me any more than it did to the rocks at my feet or the stump I leaned against. My consciousness was just idling.

Something changed. A doe had materialized on the other side of the stream. In the half-light, she was almost invisible. I didn't move. She sniffed the air, seeming to sense danger nearby. I didn't move.

She stood at the edge of the stream – almost like a paper target. Awestruck, I watched her. Questing for the scent or sound of danger, she moved her head slightly from side to side. I just watched. As she lowered her head toward the muddy water, I remembered that I was supposed to be hunting.

In slow motion I raised the rifle. She tensed. I froze. Her muscles quivered. She was ready to bolt for sure. I steadied the front sight on her chest just behind the shoulder at the same time drawing back the hammer to full cock. I don't remember squeezing the trigger or feeling the heavy kick of the rifle against my shoulder.

When I opened my eyes – I must have closed them before I fired – my ears rang and the doe was down. She struggled for a moment trying to get up, but couldn't get her legs under her. I worked the action of the rifle to be ready for a second shot – allowing a wounded animal to run off and die in the brush somewhere was a cardinal sin in the code that even the drunken men back at camp observed.

I didn't need to shoot her again. Her legs twitched a few more times, then she lay still. Her buck and the rest of the tribe abandoned her. I could hear them crashing off through the brush.

A dozen hesitant steps brought me to the edge of the stream where I could see her clearly. Her huge brown eyes were open but no breath stirred her chest. She lay still. Her tongue stuck out the corner of her mouth like she was concentrating on a really difficult problem. But she would never solve it. She would never again do anything, run or eat or give birth. Time paused for me as we regarded each other in this rude chapel. Did I apologize? I don't know. Did I cry? I think so.

Heart pounding, I crossed the stream and stood over her. What was I to do now?

As if in answer to my silent cry for help, from upstream came the sound of heavy bodies thrashing through the brush and a voice yelling, "Paddy! Paddy, where are you?" then the screech of a police whistle. It had to be the Old Man.

I dug out my whistle and blew it in answer, but stayed with my doe. Eventually the Old Man burst out of the brush on the other side of the stream, followed shortly by my Uncle Connor with a whistle in his mouth. Why had they been so far upstream? Did he start drinking and forget where he left his kid?

As it turned out, that's exactly what happened. He and my uncle had been searching farther upstream for nearly an hour. Before they went back to camp to raise a larger search party, they'd decided to work downstream a little to see if they'd come across me. The gunshot brought them to investigate.

My old man walked over to the deer, pushed the body with his foot, then looked at me. "Damn, Boy," and shook his head.

"What were you planning to do, Paddy? She needs to be dressed out or some of the meat will spoil," said Uncle Connor.

"I don't…I wasn't sure…"

"Come on over here and I'll guide you." He looked at the Old Man and asked, "unless you want to teach him, George." The Old Man was clearly not interested. He shook his head and lit a cigarette.

"You're going to start by making a vee cut just below her breast bone, right about here" he said, jabbing me in the chest. His eyes landed on my rifle where I'd left it propped against a tree. "Damn it, Paddy! What in the hell were you thinking?" He grabbed me by the shoulder and shoved me over to the tree. "Is there a round in the chamber?" When I nodded yes, he snatched up the rifle, "And it's at full cock ready to fire. That's how people get killed, Boy!" He fired it in the air. "Just that easy." He tossed it to me. "Unload it, and make sure there's no chance of anyone getting shot accidentally."

"Give him a break, Connor, he was excited and wasn't thinking"

"Would that have brought either of us back from the dead if we'd stumbled over that rifle?"

Uncle Connor paced back and forth for a minute then waved me back to the doe. "Now cut along her belly pretty much where the brown fur changes to white – yeah, right there. Not too deep. You don't want to punch a hole in her guts – it'll stink to high heaven and crap up the meat. Now across the legs and up under the tail."

He looked over at the Old Man and laughed. "He's a little squeamish, George. Haven't you told him about the birds and bees?"

"I know about that. It just smells bad, that's all," I said defending my twelve-year-old dignity.

"Yeah, sure. Now you've cut the skin all the way around, just roll her over on her side and yank it and everything should come out."

I did what he told me. "Shit!" I had to jump back to avoid a wave of deer guts. Both men were laughing.

"Give me that knife, Boy," Uncle Connor said, "I'll finish up while you get some of the slime off your pants."

He took the knife from me, reached up into her chest, made a couple of cuts and pulled out her heart and lungs. "You need a bigger knife, Paddy. You keep this one nice and sharp, but the blade isn't long enough." He held a bloody, dark red chunk of meat out to me. "This is her heart. You see what your bullet did to it?"

"Yeah," I said, pretending I knew what an intact deer heart should look like.

"And look here. You got three with one shot!" He pulled me over and lifted a pink bulb about the size of a softball with a tracery of deep red threads running through it.

"You don't know what you're looking at do you?" He motioned me closer with his chin and carefully slit it open. Inside were two greyish translucent bags, each containing a little grub-like creature maybe as long as my finger. When he opened the little sacks, it was clear that each embryo had a big head, huge eyes and four leg buds pointed with tiny hooves.

Oh my god, oh my god, oh my god! I won't throw up. I won't throw up. I won't...

"She was pregnant with two fauns, Paddy!"

He laughed and placed the babies back on the pile. He squatted down beside her, silent for ten or fifteen seconds then he stood up. With his bloody finger he made two stripes on my left cheek. "You've taken your first step to manhood, Paddy."

"Jesus, Connor!" the Old Man whined, "We don't do that shit. We're not living in the jungle for crissakes!" But, he didn't tell me to wipe my face.

The three of us carried my doe back to the camp. "Your sister is going to pitch a fit if he shows up with blood on his face, you know." Uncle Connor didn't bother to say anything. He just smiled.

Back at camp, we tied a rope around her neck and hauled her carcass into a tree to cool. We propped the legs apart to let air circulate through the purplish-red bloody body cavity. She swung from the limb awkward and graceless, turning slowly one way and then the other. He stood for a moment with his hand on her side.

"Make sure you clean that damn rifle before you do anything else. Then see what you can do to rinse the blood and shit off your clothes." He lit a cigarette and walked away from the camp toward the lake.

Uncle John came out as we were finishing. Through the open door I could hear the Old Man bragging about my hunting skills and turning my twenty-five yard lucky shot into a two hundred and fifty yard proof of superior marksmanship. My uncle closed the door behind him and walked around the carcass. "Connor help you clean her?" I nodded.

"A clean one-shot kill," he looked at me and the marks on my cheek. "Good." He followed Uncle Connor down to the lake.

I've never killed for sport again.

Ice Fishing

I was thirteen when my Old Man and his buddies discovered ice fishing. The group, laughingly referred to as the Raggedy-Assed Sportsmen's Club, was made up of about a dozen men loosely related to each other, including my Old Man, two of my uncles and a cousin. Following family tradition, there were no dues or bylaws or any discernable organization structure, just a deep commitment to spending weekends in some outdoor sport followed by incisive intellectual questions – the most common of which was "How much beer is left?"

I served as club mascot – not sure how that happened – none of the other sons ever joined us. Perhaps there was only one slot available, or maybe my cousins were smart enough to find other things to do. As mascot, I was responsible for fetching and carrying, splitting wood, cleaning fish and keeping the fire going during RASC outings.

Not having a wife to hide from, I didn't completely understand the members' desperate need to fill the gap between the end of duck season in December and the opening day of fishing season in April. It was clearly a project of high priority and the subject of the meeting this coming weekend.

"Paddy," the Old Man said that Wednesday night shortly after Christmas, "get the ice fishing traps out of the back seat of the car, will you? We need to be sure they're set up for this weekend."

Ice fishing? Traps? Who went ice fishing? Some dope in a little hut fishing through a hole in the ice? Ridiculous. Where were they going to find a hut big enough to fit the poker table? And, what would an ice fishing trap look like – some kind of scaled-down lobster pot?

Sure enough, when I got out to the car, there were two bundles of sticks sitting on the carpet of empty beer bottles in the back. Each bundle held a half-dozen or so smaller bundles that were bolted together somehow. Maybe you had to put them together like an airplane model or something? Their function wasn't any clearer to me when I got them into the kitchen.

"You see how these work, Paddy?" The Old Man took out one of the mysterious wooden contraptions.

I didn't admit to him that I didn't "get it". On the end of one stick there was a cheesy reel and some line but these were somehow used in fishing?

The Old Man proceeded to twist the sticks around. "These make a cross that keeps the trap from falling through the ice." Another twist. "And this holds the reel and the flag. You bait your hook, drop your line through the hole, then bend this down and latch it here."

The whippy piece of steel with its bright red flag snapped up and hit him right across the face, sending his cigarette flying and leaving an angry-looking welt. "Damn it!" he yelped and bent to retrieve the Old Gold burning its way into the linoleum. "That could have put my eye out." He glared at me waiting for me to laugh, then surrendered to laughter himself. "You want to be careful when you hook the flag, Boy. You could get hurt." And he laughed some more.

We fiddled with the traps for another twenty minutes – long enough for me to get somewhat familiar with these new devices and a little tired of being stung by mishaps with the flags. "After you put the line in and set the flag, then what?" I asked.

"When a fish takes the bait, the flag snaps up to let you know what's happened," he lit another cigarette, "and then you send the boy out to haul in the fish and reset the trap."

Now I understood the attraction of ice fishing. The men could sit in the nice warm cabin playing poker and drinking, while the fish caught themselves. "The Boy" would then be detailed to retrieve the dumb fish. This was a better invention than the pop top. The only discomfort the members might endure was getting the hole cut in the first place – I suspected "The Boy" would have a role in that as well.

But, what would you need a dozen traps for? Even the greediest surf casters down at the beach didn't try to use more than two rods at a time. I got my answer that weekend.

That Saturday we set out. "Help me put the chains on the car, Paddy." The Old Man handed me a tangled mess of rusty chain and cleats. "Lay one out flat behind each rear wheel – no, you've got it upside down – let me know when I'm about half way over them." He backed the car up so the chains were under the wheels, then showed me how to hook the ends together around the tires. "Okay, Boy, you finish up."

Shoving my head and arms into the dripping, slush-covered wheel well, I got the first chain hooked. Fifteen minutes of numb-fingered effort completed the job. The Old Man inspected my work, had me tighten the driver's side, then attached the springs that kept the chains form slapping around too much. "Go on inside and clean up and we'll head out."

He drove slowly – not that the old coupe was likely to break any speed records – on dry roads the chains made an incredible clatter.

"Dad, won't the chains cut into the tires?" I didn't drive yet, but running your tires over big hunks of metal looked like a sure way to get a flat. And I was pretty sure who'd end up changing the damn snow-covered tire.

"Nah," he said, "just got to be careful."

He let me turn the radio up and listen to that "yeah, yeah, yeah shit" as he described it, so I was content to wait and see what happened. Once we got away from the coast and started climbing into the mountains, the roads were snow-covered and the chains quieted down – he didn't make me turn the radio down though.

At the last steep hill up to the cabin, he swerved off the road, rumbled across a field, and into the lake! We're going to drown! I screamed and was dragging at the door handle ready to jump, and he just laughed at my terror. We didn't end up *in* the lake, but *on* it. We were driving a car on the ice. We didn't fall through.

"How did you know that the ice would hold a car?" I asked, thunderstruck. Memories of falling through the ice on Higgins' Pond surfaced. My idiot friends and I tried to hurry the hockey season and I damn near drowned.

Casual drag on his cigarette. "Didn't" he said, as we reached a spot on the ice below the cabin. "Leave the traps and the bucket here and take the other stuff inside."

By the time I'd broken a trail through the two-foot deep snow and lugged the beer and food up the hill, my uncles had arrived, and I had more stuff to carry. My Uncle John, at least, helped.

A few more club members arrived, turning the lake in front of our cabin into a parking lot. Everyone was settling in for an afternoon of poker, I was reading my book when some idiot piped up, "when are we going to go fishing?" The voice sounded a lot like mine.

The bass grumbling and comments about "colder than a well-digger's ass" and "freeze the balls off a brass monkey" had a certain resignation to them. The men knew that in order to conjure "ice fishing" from "sitting around playing poker and drinking" for the benefit of the later story to the wives, an effort to complete the ritual had to be made. Since it was a new sport for the club, no one was sure what minimum level of performance was necessary to accomplish the transformation. But surely setting some traps was required.

"Okay, Paddy, we'll go fishing," said Uncle Connor. He, Danny Sawyer and his cousin Charlie, and I pulled on our hats and coats and trudged out to the cars. The rest of the group wandered as far as the lake shore behind us – making sure that they had full beers before embarking on the trek – then returned to the cabin.

We piled into one of the cars and drove a couple of hundred yards farther onto the frozen lake, stopping a spot Uncle John picked. After unloading the traps and bait pails, we spread out to set the traps. As I had guessed, I was handed an ice chisel.

"Make the holes about a foot across and maybe ten yards apart," Uncle John directed. He nodded to where the cousins were working, Charlie chopping and Danny setting the traps, "and stay out of their way. Connor and I will follow you and set up the traps."

At first chopping through the ice was pretty easy – the ice chisel, a six-foot piece of pipe with a three-inch chisel blade welded to one end, was heavy and sharp enough to cut through the ice quickly. After the first two holes, the chisel got heavier and heavier. After half a dozen holes, I was ready to add the ice chisel to my personal hall of fame for torture instruments.

While the five-degree air sandpapered my throat and lungs and made my teeth hurt, my heavy cold-weather gear trapped the heat from my exertions causing me to drip with sweat inside my clothes. It was no wonder that the ice could hold up a car, it was more than fifteen inches thick, requiring stroke after stroke of the damn chisel to get through.

I could hear Danny yelling to his cousin, "Put some muscle into it, Charlie. I'm freezing my ass off out here" Apparently I wasn't the only one running out of energy.

Uncle Connor came up and took the chisel out of my hands. "We need to keep moving, Paddy. I'll spell you for a while." He quickly chopped half a dozen holes, while I set the traps and shivered in my freezing wet undershirt.

Finally Connor yelled over to Danny, "That ought to be enough, don't you think?" Danny nodded and finished setting his traps. Danny, Connor and I scrambled back into the idling car. Warmth, finally! I couldn't stop shivering.

Charlie got into the car, sat for a minute then looked back at Danny. "Well?"

"Well what?" Danny frowned and pointed out at the spread of traps. "We wait for a bite."

"I ain't gonna sit here in this damn car and wait for the damn fish to show up," Charlie muttered. "I'm going back up to the cabin and get a beer." He stomped back toward the cabin over the ice on foot. Uncle Connor looked at Danny, then put the car in gear and followed Charlie.

For the next hour I lost myself in Richard S. Prather with an occasional look out the window to see how our fishing was going. I was warm and dozing, listening to the wind whistling around the eaves and the crackle of the fire, grateful to be out of the cold

"Paddy, we got a bite." The Old Man barked. "Go see if we caught anything."

"George," responded Charlie, "that's a long damn way to walk in the wind and all. He's done his duty, let him be."

The Old Man turned to my uncle, "Connor, did you leave the keys in my car?" Uncle Connor nodded that he had.

The Old Man turned back to me. "Okay, Paddy, you can take the car."

Neither of my uncles were in favor. "Are you sure he's old enough, George?" Uncle John chimed in.

"Yeah. It's time he learned."

He turned back to me and repeated, "Paddy, take the car. You'll have to choke it a little to get it started, but don't flood it."

I was going to drive! This ice fishing business was going to be great! "Paddy, take the car," he said – damn! Visions of how cool I'd look piloting the car around the ice – "yeah, I do this all the time, Babe, hop in." Where I thought the ice fishing bunnies would come from was left open. This will be great, maybe I can be the driver all the time when we're up here. I was barely able to lace up my boots my hands were shaking so badly. "Be back in a few minutes," I said over my shoulder, trying to be casual – sure, I drive all over the place, didn't you know?

The ice cold driver's seat and steering wheel couldn't cool my enthusiasm. Driving, so cool! Driving on a frozen lake, even cooler! Well, I wasn't going very far if I didn't adjust the seat – I could barely touch the pedals. After years of driving in the same position, the seat latch was corroded in place. I fumbled and yanked and threw my weight back against the seat until it released – and slammed all the way back accompanied by the clash of the empty bottles. A few more lunges and pulls on the lever got the seat up as far as it would go. Now I could see over the steering wheel – if I stretched my neck a little. Okay, need to choke it a little – where in the hell is the choke? Oh, there it is. How much is a little? Did he mean give it full choke for a little while or pull the choke out less than all the way? I'll pull it out half way and see what happens.

I turned the ignition key and was rewarded with a cheerful glow from the dash lights and the hum of the heater fan. Here we go. Just push the silver starter button and….

Blam! The steering wheel reared back and smacked me in the nose, the horn blared and the car leaped backward and stalled. What…what….what the hell happened? Did some invisible force suddenly attack the car? My nose was bleeding like a faucet and it hurt like hell. The car was stalled, probably with irreparable damage. And I was going have to slink back up to camp and explain it all.

Then it hit me – the *clutch*. I was concentrating so hard on the choke, I forgot to push in the clutch. Like most standard transmission drivers, Uncle Connor ignored the parking brake and just left the car in reverse. With the car in gear, it won't move and you saved an unnecessary step. If it hadn't stalled, the car would have rocketed backwards across the lake until it hit something. *That* would have been really tough to explain.

Clutch in, choke half way out, punch the starter and there we are, the little six-cylinder clicking and rattling away up front. The clutch sort of got away from me again after I pulled the lever down into first and started off. Stalled again. Kick in the clutch. Try again. Easy. Easy. We're moving!

I chugged over to the traps my bloody hands leaving evidence on the steering wheel. Tried to stop. Oh, no one mentioned that you have to pump the brakes. Ran over a trap. Stalled it again. The hell with it. Turned off the key.

Ice Fishing

With shaking legs, I left the car and walked over to the trap that had been sprung. Damn, the hole had iced over! Can't pull a fish up through a half-inch of ice. Back to the car to get the ice chisel. I cleared out the hole, carefully avoiding the jerking and wiggling line. We definitely had caught something. The line kept slipping through my gloves so I had to take them off and pull in the line bare-handed.

The fish's movements became more frantic as I got it closer to the surface. There he was! A long streamlined body, dark green on top with red tipped fins – a nice big pickerel.

I got him up on the ice, tried to hold him and get the hook out with numb hands – the sonofabitch bit me – hard. My left thumb had slid into his mouth while I twisted out the hook with my right hand. He clamped down and wouldn't let go! He was getting even for every fish sandwich I'd ever eaten.

The skin of my thumb gave way and the fish flopped back on the ice. I gave him a good kick to remind him who's at the top of the food chain – then watched, horrified, as he slid in slow motion across the ice and plopped back down the hole.

Now my thumb was bleeding from the pickerel attack, my nose was still bleeding from the assault by the steering wheel and I'd lost the damn fish! Maybe I should just dive down the hole with the pickerel. Then I heard my Uncle Connor laughing.

"Guess you showed him, Paddy."

I wiped both tears and blood out of my eyes to see both he and Uncle John leaning against the car having clearly witnessed my battle with the leviathan.

Uncle John was shaking with laughter and struggling for breath. When he'd gotten some control over himself, he did a mincing little sissy kick, like a hippo doing ballet, then imitated the inexorable path of the fish back to the hole, and convulsed with

19

laughter again. Then he walked over to me, put his arm around my shoulders and walked me toward the car.

"Come on, Boy, it could have been worse …it could have been a bigger fish." He paused, "You want to drive back?"

"No," I answered stiffly. They must have seen my driving exhibition as well – great!

Uncle Connor joined us. "Paddy, this one of the traps you set?"

"Yeah…I guess. I did most of them on this end," grudgingly forcing my voice out.

"Did you use the minnows from the bucket as bait?"

"Well…yeah, wasn't I supposed to?"

"You put a minnow on the hook." He started laughing again. "That's the problem."

"Huh?" Crap! I screwed up something else. "Is there some other bait I was supposed to use?"

"Not exactly." I could hear Uncle John was snickering in the background. "No one else used any bait."

"No bait? How can you catch a fish without bait?"

The two men hovered over me. "Paddy, don't be dumb. Do you really like standing out here in the cold with a ten-knot wind blowing to pull in a fish you have no intention of eating?"

"And that bites," Uncle John felt compelled to throw in.

"Ah…well…I dunno…" I stammered

"The smart hunter knows what he's going after. We only catch the fish that are stupid…or suicidal." Then I got it.

All in all it was a pretty good weekend. I got to drive a car on a frozen lake, caught a fish (that would grow with retelling), and went back to school with two black eyes and a swollen nose. The big bandage on my hand guaranteed me lots chances to tell (and embellish) my story.

Best of all, the Technicolor bruises also improved my position in high school from a lowly freshman to an *interesting* lowly freshman – didn't get the upper class girls to talk to me though – apparently not the right bait.

Royal Enfield

It was over ninety degrees and the heat radiating off the pavement made it worse. The wicked motorcycles that Billy found better be something special. Not that I had anything better to do, but I was roasting in my regulation black leather jacket and brylcreme-pasted pompadour.

Billy was more widely traveled than I, and often ventured across the bridge into what was enemy territory for a wannabe thug.

"They're English bikes," he enthused, "used in the war. And one even has a sidecar."

"Wicked!" I responded – it was our stock exclamation. Like all teenage secret languages, it had many meanings and sometimes no meaning at all, just a space filler.

We were both sixteen that summer, had our driver's licenses but had little hope of acquiring a car. We'd been friends since we were about ten. We didn't live in the same part of town – Billy's father owned a big boat building and repair business down to the Point. Billy often stayed with his grandfather, who lived just up the street from me, on a lot of weekends and school vacations. We met, had a fist fight, then started hanging out together.

He appealed to my wilder side and we both studied to develop a suitably dangerous – and mysterious – hoodlum image. He didn't mind that I was a little bit chicken and would rather avoid a fight than start one. We ran together, occasionally joined by other malcontents, until I got a Princeton haircut and joined the preppy crowd halfway through high school.

"So what kind of bikes are these?" I asked "You said they were English. Like BSA or Triumph?" The thought of blasting around town on a Triumph Bonneville was enough to cause me to forget my practiced insolent sneer.

"Royal Enfield. That's a big motorcycle company over there."

"Enfield, like the Enfield rifle?"

"It's the same name," Billy snapped, "how the hell would I know if it's the same company?" He hesitated for a minute. "They do look like they might be Army motorcycles, though. Painted green and all."

When we got to Izzy's, I was overwhelmed by the sheer size of the place. It was an old mill building along the harbor crammed full of cars, car parts, tractors, trucks and the universe of pieces that made them run. If you didn't have a wheel puller or the right bodyman's dolly, it was likely you could find what you needed in one of the heaps in between the recognizable hulks. For Billy and I, and kids like us, Izzy's was a treasure house of unrealized potential. Izzy had hot rods waiting to be built. The front fender for the '49 Chevy you were trying to get on the road. Or, the outboard motor that would transform your twelve-foot skiff into a speedboat. In short, it was a junkyard.

It was also a four-mile walk from home and a known hang-out for hot rodders and other ne'er-do-wells.

We were met in the front office by Izzy. He was a man singularly ill-favored by the gods, about five foot five in all dimensions, ears like flags flying out from the sides of his head, a nose like a potato, and rotten teeth.

Around his cigarette, this vision mumbled, "back to see those Limey bikes, huh, Billy?" He looked over at a couple of guys listening to the Red Sox game on the radio, "You better buy 'em pretty quick before someone else gets them." He let out a bray that would have impressed my grandfather's mule, which I took to be laughter. "Go on back, you know where they are. Fifty bucks each or the two of 'em for seventy-five."

Both of them for seventy-five dollars? Billy told me that we'd each need fifty bucks. Wicked! A bargain!

Up against the wall behind the frame and most of the coachwork for a pre-war Lincoln Continental were two of the sorriest-looking motorcycles I had ever seen. Leaning against each other like two drunks, they were covered in dust and cobwebs, with an old lawnmower and what appeared to be the hood of a Nash piled on top of them.

"Billy, these things won't ever run. They're just scrap!"

"Ran when he brought 'em in here," Izzy was standing behind me, thumb comfortably hooked in the belt that was apparently holding up his belly as well as his pants. I didn't have the nerve to ask if we were still fighting the Kaiser at the time.

"Yep, said he got them when he was stationed in England. Rode them for a while over here then parked 'em." He stepped over and inspected the bikes. "Excellent machines, used them all over the world, they did. Those are both 350 WD-C models – the WD stands for War Department. See that emblem? Built like a gun it says"

It was a wicked emblem, a picture of a cannon with that motto below it and Royal Enfield above.

Billy looked at me. "What do you think?"

"About what? These things look like they've been sitting forever. They're probably all seized up and we'll never get parts." I shook my head in disgust. "Wouldn't mind having the emblem though."

"You the mechanic then, boy?" Izzy asked me.

"I guess."

"There's some tools in the office. Whyn't you use 'em to actually check them out?" challenged Izzy.

In fairness to Izzy, the bikes were filthy beyond belief, but appeared to still have all of their parts. Using the merchant's tools, I removed the spark plug from the first bike and had Billy crank it. I even got a faint spark between the plug wire and the head. This one might run after all. We put it up on the side stand and played with the transmission, which also seemed to be free. The tires and brakes were bad, but maybe…

Billy got on my case, "wasn't as bad as you thought, huh, smart ass?"

Izzy had left after we got the toolbox so I was confident asking Billy, "you think he'd let us try to get it started before we buy it?"

"Yeah, then he'll sell it to some sailor for a couple of hundred!"

I heard heavy feet coming up behind us as we argued. "Look, Billy, I put up with your shit because of your brother. Either buy it now and don't bother to come back here again…ever." Salesmanship Izzy style.

Billy looked at me. I faced Izzy and sucked up my courage. "Both of them for sixty dollars cash."

"You little shit! Who the hell do you think you are?" I could feel the saliva of his indignation. "Sixty bucks? I'm not sure I'll sell even one of them for that."

I wiped off his tools and started returning them to the box.

"Where do you live?" We told him. "Okay, seventy-five and I'll deliver them. Deal?"

Billy spoke up, "Fifty now and the last twenty-five when you deliver them."

A few days later, Izzy's truck pulled into Nelson's Yard and dropped off the two motorcycles. Billy's father and his brother, Hank, strolled over and started laughing.

"Shit, Boy," Hank crowed, "you coulda just give me the seventy-five dollars and I wouldna even screwed ya."

I thought of Billy's father as the Giant – not just that he was tall, he was big everywhere. His hands were as big as my head. His voice was like rocks rolling down a river valley – not quite human. He looked at the bikes then put his paw on Billy's shoulder. "This is going to be an expensive lesson, Son. Now I'd like you and your friend here to move your junk out of the middle of my driveway."

We humped the bikes over to a little shed and pushed the one with the side car – the one that Billy'd claimed – inside.

"I'll borrow my Old Man's truck and come back for the other one as soon as I can," I said, hoping that I'd be able to get the truck.

The Old Man was not pleased. "You bought a motorcycle? Does it run? Who'd you get it from? What makes you think you're going to ride a motorcycle, anyway?"

"Well, Billy and I..."

"Billy who?"

"Billy Nelson, we found these two bikes at Izzy's…"

"Jeeeesus Christ! Are you really that damn stupid? You know that the whole family is a bunch a jailbirds, right? Hell, isn't Hank still in prison?"

"He got out a couple of months…"

"I don't give a shit! And the Nelsons have you trading at Izzy's? Another damn jailbird! Did you get a title or a bill of sale or anything? How do you know these motorcycles aren't stolen?"

"Well, a guy in the Air Force brought them back from England and…"

"Stop right there." He glared at me. Lit a cigarette. Glared some more. "Where were you planning to work on this motorcycle? It doesn't run does it?"

"No, I thought I could put it behind the station and work on it when there's no one around."

"You know what I should do, don't you? I should pay a visit to Mr. Isadore Flynn and shake him upside down until your money falls out. I might still do that." More glaring. "No, you'll learn a lesson this way, dummy."

I didn't ask him about using the truck, I just grabbed the bike the next time I working at the station and went out for parts – couldn't be any more pissed off than he was already, right?

Thankfully, he wasn't at the station when I arrived with the motorcycle. Rip Shea strolled over to help me unload it. He was the Old Man's top mechanic and a part-time race driver who loved to refer to me as the *nepotee* since I was the boss's kid. Rip walked all the way around the bike, squatted down and checked the engine, jiggled the brake and shift levers. "Royal Enfield, huh?" reading the side plates.

He stood up and pronounced, "Well, everything's here." Then he walked back into the shop.

The Old Man forbade me bringing the Enfield into the shop when any work was going on, which meant I could work on it at night and Sundays when only the pumps were open. That also meant that I had to move a three-hundred pound motorcycle with flat tires all the way around the building every time I wanted to work on it. Getting it in condition so I could roll it rather than drag it was critical.

"What the hell size is this supposed to be?" the counterman at the tire store frowned and was frankly looking for a better customer than a sixteen-year old kid.

Having anticipated problems, I whipped out the dry-rotted tube that came out of the Enfield's tire and showed him the designation. "It's an English tire," I offered.

"Looks like you'll have to go to England to get a tube, Sonny." He walked off down the counter.

"Hey kid, lemme see that," another counter guy walked over and took the tube out of my hands. "Look, kid. This says that it's for a three and half inch width on a twenty-inch rim – that sound about right? In those days there were no low profile tires – the height of the tire is the same as the rim width."

He went back into the shelves and returned with two tubes. "Got a restoration project going, huh?" When I agreed, he continued. "Ariel?"

"No, Royal Enfield, 350"

He opened one of the boxes and stretched the tube out on top of the old one. It was pretty much the same. "When you're ready for tires, come back. We'll probably have to try some things to get everything just right – won't have as much leeway as with a tube."

Two nights of fiddling got both tires inflated and installed. My project no longer included a test of strength. The next day was Saturday so the shop closed at noon and I'd have all afternoon to work on the Enfield.

"You know you can't shine shit, right?" Rip had backed his stock car on the trailer into the shop. Before he started tuning it for the races later, he watched me scrubbing and scraping to get the Enfield clean. We were both taking advantage of the shop being available for personal projects after my Old Man left for the weekend. I still had to sell gas, but the Old Man set prices high enough that I didn't have to be too concerned about heavy volume.

"Just got tired of not being able to see what I was doing," I answered.

"With your mechanical skill, nepotee, it doesn't matter. That thing ain't ever gonna run.

Rip lit up the race car and conversation was no longer possible. With its hopped up engine and straight pipes it was deafening and had to be revved up to stay running. According to Rip, low-class cars like his – he was running a '56 Plymouth with the 272 cubic-inch V-8 – just ran in second gear all the way around the half-mile dirt track. "Just keep the revs up to about forty-five-hundred on the straights and let off a little in the corners and you can just slide all the way around."

Eventually, he was satisfied with the car and shut it down. Blessed silence.

He walked over to where I was working. "Where are you at with this, anyway?"

"The motor's free, I've got good spark. I took the tank off and cleaned it out as well as I could and replaced the gas line as far as the fuel shut off. The couple of times I've tried it, it won't fire. Guess I need to clean the carburetor."

30

"Let's try something." He walked over to the other side of the shop and grabbed the five-gallon gas can we used for road service and handed it to me. "Squirt a gallon of gas in the tank, Sonny. We'll see if this piece of shit will run."

When I returned, he had me dribble a small amount of gas into the mouth of the carburetor.

"Turn it on and kick it."

As instructed, I stomped on the kick starter half a dozen times. The Enfield barked once, backfired and quit.

"Alright, Mr. Nepotee, what do you think?"

"I think we've flooded it."

"What should we do?"

Rip's Socratic method was beginning to get on my nerves. "Let it sit for a few minutes, open the throttle and try to start it – see if it will dump the extra gas. Then try again."

"So that's what we'll do. Oh, you've got a customer. Your father would be very disappointed if you didn't take care of him right away." He pointed out to the pumps. "And, be sure to check the oil," he tossed after me as I scooted out to the pumps.

The second try with the Enfield didn't go any better than the first.

"Well, Boy, I can't spend all afternoon fixing your motorcycle for you. But..." He walked over to his bench and brought a spray can back. "Stand beside it this time when you try to start it."

"Rip, it's flooded."

He used the can to spray the throat of the carburetor. "Try it," he ordered.

I stood on the right-hand side of the bike, cranked the throttle open, and shoved the starter lever down with my left foot. The bike exploded into life – the motor revving up like there was no tomorrow.

"Let off on the throttle, dummy!" Rip shouted over the roar.

I did and the bike settled into a rough, but sustained idle – then it quit.

"Yeah," Rip noted, "gonna have to clean the carburetor." He walked over to his truck and trailer. "No charge for the ether. Just buy me coffee in the morning."

Ether – I could smell it now – it's what they used to start big diesel trucks in cold weather. No wonder he didn't want me astride the damn bike – it could have gone up in flames under me!

Cleaning the carb was painstaking but fairly straight forward. The transmission however beat me. I had the bike to the point where it would start and run in neutral, but the minute I tried to put it in gear, it locked up and quit. I fiddled around, trying lubrication, rocking the shift lever, even pulling off the side cases and applying some force. It was frozen and I was done. I considered asking Rip – or even the Old Man – for advice, but I knew what I'd hear. "I told you it was a piece of shit. Why did you waste your money? Maybe you should call an English mechanic. Etc."

I hitch-hiked down to the boatyard to see if Billy had made any better progress with his Enfield. I found him under a cradle holding a big Novi lobster boat. He had WMEX turned up so loud that his little transistor radio was distorting. He was singing along with Eric Burton and scraping the crud off the boat's bottom, oblivious of the rest of the world.

"Hey!" I shouted. "What the hell are you doing?"

He jumped, banged his head, swore, then crawled out. "What the hell does it look like, dumbass? I'm working." He looked around and dropped the scraper. "you got a smoke?"

I lit mine and shook out one for him and threw him the lighter. "Looks like a shit job."

He took a deep drag. "Yup, I've gotta get this bitch scraped and painted by the weekend so we can put her over. Hank's gonna tow her up to Whitey's for a tune-up Saturday."

"Doesn't look like you're gonna make it, man," I said looking at the bottom of the boat. "You need help?"

"Whaddaya think?"

"Gimme a scraper and I'll start at the stern."

Between us we managed to get all the weed, barnacles, and old anti-fouling paint off her. Billy only had one electric sander so we took turns swallowing the dust and grit getting her bottom smooth enough for paint.

During a break we took a look at Billy's Enfield which appeared unchanged from the day we dragged it into the shed.

"Haven't had a chance to work on it much, huh?" I offered.

"Naw, I put a new plug and some gas in it – sonofabitch just won't start. I kicked it until my crotch was sore, but no dice." He borrowed another cigarette. "I think we're gonna use it as an anchor for a new mooring," he said nonchalantly.

"No, really?"

"What else?"

I had an idea that would solve two problems for me. A few weeks ago I'd finally found a girl who would go out with me. I had discovered that the seething, drooling and slavering lust that lay just beneath my polished exterior put most girls off – I suppose it could be the Clearasil scent, too. Anyway, Cindy had gone to the movies with me and had allowed me to kiss her and make out a little. A long way from home, but there was hope.

The problem with having a girlfriend is that they expect you to spend time with them – and not watching while you screw around with a *dirty, old motorcycle*. They also expected to go places – and with a reasonably well-dressed boyfriend. All of this spelled M-O-N-E-Y, and the Enfield was taking, not giving.

"Billy, I'd sell you my bike for fifty bucks. It's running, the brakes work okay, all it needs is new rubber." Generations of sharp-dealing fisherman looked out of his eyes. "'course we'd have to swap the transmission from yours."

"It actually runs, but the transmission's bad?"

"Yeah, it took a while to get the timing right, but now it starts right up in neutral. The damn transmission is frozen solid – I'm afraid of bending the crank if I keep trying to force it into gear." He still looked skeptical. "I'll even help you swap it out. Whaaddaya think?"

"Fifty bucks? Why should you make a profit on me?"

"Make a profit – you're kidding."

"No, you paid thirty-seven-fifty for it, same's I did. And that was only a month and a half ago."

Billy can suddenly do arithmetic! When in the hell did that happen? "Bill, I put parts into it and hours and it's *running*! That ought to be worth something."

"Why don't you give me fifty dollars for mine, then? I put parts and labor into it."

I gave up. "I need the money and, besides, the Old Man won't let me register it, even if I could fix the transmission. Once he saw that I had it running, he laid down the law."

"So you gotta sell it," Billy said triumphantly.

His hard-headedness got to me. "Jesus Christ! I just spent four frigging hours helping you out of a jam…for nothing. And, you want to screw me out of a couple of bucks? That stinks!"

"Okay," he said, "you did help. Not much of a boat builder, but you did help. Fifty it is – but you gotta help me swap my transmission into your bike."

"Deal."

That Sunday, we moved my Enfield down to the boatyard in the shop's truck and began stripping pieces of Billy's bike and replacing the ones on mine. Another week and we had a vehicle that would actually move under its own power. Some kind of an alignment problem made getting it into first gear uncertain, but we could get it rolling in second with a little clutch slipping and then it worked as it should.

"I'll write to the company, " I offered, "and see if they'll sell me a shop manual or something so we can get first to work every time. It'll probably take quite a while though." I did write to the company in Redditch, England, as promised, but didn't hear anything back.

The fifty dollars came in very handy – allowing me to upgrade my wardrobe to a level suitable for squiring a young lady around. I didn't get any further than light making out with her even with the new duds. This was probably okay. Deep down, I think I was a little frightened of making a fool of myself and eliminating any chance of a sex life…ever.

I saw Billy on the Enfield once after I sold it to him. He was sitting on it in front of the Greeks, kind of a coffee shop that also sold beer and magazines. A general hang out for us.

"Jesus, Bill, you're not riding on those old tires – you'll get killed." The bikes tires were the same old dry-rotted ones that I'd just put new tubes in.

"They're fine for now," he said.

They weren't.

> *Springfield Argosy* – August 17, 1964 - A 16-year old was killed on route 3 on Monday. According to the State Police, William Nelson of Canton lost control of his motorcycle while passing another car and crashed into an oncoming vehicle. Nelson was pronounced dead at the scene. According to Sergeant Toomey of the New Hampshire State Police, Nelson's vintage motorcycle was traveling at a high rate of speed at the time of the crash. "We will not be able to establish a definite cause until a complete investigation has been made. Certainly speed was a factor, but the vehicle was also quite old and mechanical failure can't be ruled out.

A day or two after Billy's funeral, a letter arrived with a beautiful English stamp. It was from Royal Enfield thanking me for my interest and informing me that Enfield's parts department would happily send me a complete service manual for the WD-C. I should enclose a draft for fifteen pounds sterling with my order.

To Be Cool

Taking risks to find your place in life is key to growing up – or not growing up.

Teddy and I competed for academic recognition all through junior high and high school. He was certainly as smart as I was and had, what I considered an unfair advantage, an excellent work ethic. I daydreamed and drifted through school – it was a pleasant place to go, chat with people and hear about all kinds of new things. The new things – algebra, geometry and literature, and such – were fascinating, but not worth any energy. I got great grades anyway, so why bother?

On the other hand, Teddy would dig and dig and dig. There was always some new fact or process or concept that he rooted out of the material I floated over. Since we were in a school that didn't really challenge him, all the effort he put in was self-motivated. His industry and intelligence made him the darling of the teachers. His slight stature, thick glasses, and habit of avoiding eye contact when speaking, pushed him to the social fringes of the tribe.

My minimal ability to play football saved me from joining Teddy in the outer darkness. Utterly ignorant of social conventions, with no money, and little knowledge of the larger world, I had none of the attributes that move one up in the dog-eat-dog social hierarchy of high school. Connection with the other players on the team – popular boys all – provided provisional status in the inner circles.

A word about playing football. Just as our high school was too small and diverse to challenge Teddy academically, it was too small and too diverse to gather a full football squad of talented players. Our team was built around half a dozen guys with actual athletic ability and the rest of us. Unlike Teddy, I was big enough to play and was encouraged to play by my Old Man.

"Get out there and knock people down," he ordered. "Show 'em you got guts." He saw football as the mid-Century American version of going out alone to kill your first lion.

My desire to gain his approval overcame the obvious risks of playing. The chief one being the likelihood of demonstrating in front of my classmates my utter lack of coordination. Although being knocked senseless by some two-hundred-fifty-pound walking glandular condition, did figure into my thinking. As long as I could run faster, I would never quit the team.

The coaches' summary: "…well, he tries."

When Teddy showed up at try outs for the track team – the football team used track as spring practice – most of us were dumbfounded. Why was he here? Gym shorts and a tee shirt just emphasized his skinny little body. The silence of the cut-down artists and mockers was a measure of how unnatural his presence seemed. If a deer had walked out of the woods, pulled on a tee shirt and spikes, and got down in the blocks for the hundred-yard dash, we couldn't have been more surprised.

I went over to Teddy, "Hey, man, what event are you thinking about?"

"Distance, I think. Maybe the mile, but more likely the two-mile.

"The two mile? That's a killer – I don't think we've ever had anyone who was any good at that distance." I didn't mention the mile, since I considered myself the best miler on the team.

"We haven't," he said. "I checked. We've never won a first in the two mile race."

Well now, didn't that figure.

"I've been running five to eight miles every day since Christmas, so I think I can do it pretty easily."

"You've been running since Christmas? In the snow?" I gasped. I'd just quit smoking for track season a week ago! He's been preparing for three months? I had to keep him out of the mile.

At our first meet, Teddy got creamed. He had the endurance, but no speed at all. I didn't do so hot either. We both got better as the season progressed. I assumed my rightful place as the team's premier miler. Teddy managed to place a couple of times.

After a meet way down east, he and I sat together on the bus ride home. My distant second in the final was weighing me down. The kid that won just ran away from all of us. The pace he set was more like the time I turn in for a four-forty. At the finish line, I could barely breathe and probably would have quit on the bell lap if anyone else in the field kept up with him. I hung on and hoped he'd fall down or have a heart attack or something.

"You did pretty well this afternoon, didn't you?" I asked

"I got third," he answered. "I didn't get tired. I just can't run fast enough to win"

"You got those short legs, man." We both laughed.

He looked up at the rack over our heads and apparently found an answer. "I think I've got to try longer distances."

Teddy quit the track team and joined the new cross-country team. Those kids were nuts! They were running as fast as they could out through the woods and puckerbrush, up and down hills, through streams and over rocks – horrible. And, there weren't even any spectators. As he had expected, Teddy did well and finished first in several races. Around school, he'd added a dimension to his image –he wasn't just the brain anymore, he was also the brain who could race ten miles through the woods in the rain and win. He became the "tough little bastid."

I don't think it got him a girlfriend, but I don't really know. Except for class, we didn't see each other much anymore.

The summer between our junior and senior years in high school, Teddy hooked up with two other guys to work at Harrison by the Sea. Summer jobs were hard to come by in our town unless your Old Man happened to draft you into the family business, and Harrison was thought to be a plum that usually went to college kids.

Harrison was a huge old resort hotel at the beach with a long veranda on the ocean side. Four stories of artistically weathered cedar shingles and cupolas, turrets and Victorian gingerbread facing five hundred yards of sandy beach and the Atlantic Ocean. In addition to your room and a world-class restaurant, there were nightly shows in the theater and a full menu of excursions and silly games. Even then it was considered a bit of an anachronism, but still managed to stay full through the entire season. Not surprisingly, the hotel had a powerful need for presentable summer help.

Although most of the kids were paid minimum wage, the Harrison was always flooded with summer job applicants. Many of the kids came back season after season. The attraction: all of the help, including the summer kids, were in residence. There was what amounted to a second hotel for the staff on the scrub land behind the resort itself. Roughly a hundred and fifty kids – girls and boys – between the ages of sixteen and twenty living together with easy access to liquor and no supervision whatsoever – teenage Disneyland!

To top it off, at the end of the season satisfactory workers got a bonus that was usually five hundred dollars. The weekly wages weren't great, but five hundred bucks all in one spot was more than most kids could earn and save over a whole summer.

Teddy, Kevin and Larry worked in the restaurants bussing dirty dishes, resetting tables and filling water glasses. They worked six days a week and usually all three meals. Even at the minimum wage of a dollar and a quarter an hour, their schedule provided them take home pay of about fifty dollars every week.

I envied Teddy. For a similar schedule at the Old Man's gas station, I took home thirty-two-twenty-seven a week – and there was no bonus in my future. And, if it was a slow week, I might have to wait a while for my pay envelope.

I envied Teddy. He lived in a building full of girls without a parent in sight. My fantasies would embarrass Hugh Hefner.

I envied Teddy. His folks gave him their old Ford station wagon so that he could come home on weekends if he wanted to. My mother's ugly damn Plymouth was available to me if I asked nicely – well in advance.

Kevin claimed it wasn't as great as I imagined.

"I live like I'm forty years old," he told me. "I get off work, come home, open a beer and sit down in front of the TV. I feel like my father!"

"What about the girls?" I asked panting to get to the good stuff.

"What about them? Sometimes we'll get some beer or something and walk down the beach away from the hotel and listen to the radio and stuff. Can't build a fire 'cause the cops will show up."

"So that's what you do? Sit on the beach drink and listen to the radio?" This was disappointing.

"What did you think?" he asked. "Orgies?"

"Well…yeah…"

"Those are only on Tuesday and Friday nights," he said and punched me in the shoulder. "Grow up, man."

Teddy and Kevin were home most weekends – Larry had a girlfriend at the hotel and didn't come home much. I was surprised, then, to see all three of them in the Greeks drinking cherry cokes and talking with the other kids.

"Teddy, I saw your Ford outside. You in for the weekend?" I asked.

His demeanor had improved over the summer. He seemed confident and…worldly? Damn, I envied Teddy.

"No, we're just here for the afternoon. Larry had something to do with his parents so we all drove up. We have to go back because Kevin and I are in the main dining room tonight."

Anxious to talk about something that didn't make me out to be such a loser, I asked, "Have you settled on a school yet?" We'd both been fortunate and were being recruited by some really good colleges. M.I.T. and Case were high on Teddy's list and I was still smarting from the cheapskate offer M.I.T made to me. I wondered if his had been better.

"Probably, M.I.T., but I like Case's nuclear engineering program. I'm down to those two."

"I'm going to Rensselaer Poly. I just sent all the crap in last week."

"Not M.I.T. ?"

"No, I didn't want to be that close to home," I fibbed.

Kevin came up and put his hand on Teddy's shoulder. "We gotta go get Larry and get moving or we'll be late," he said. "Hi, Paddy, how are you doing?"

"Just fine, Kev. Guess you guys are hurrying back to Sodom and Gomorrah, huh?"

"Yep," and the two of them walked out.

Since I was working from four-to-nine that night, I had to move along, too. I envied Teddy.

Pumping gas at a station on a road without much traffic has to be among to most boring jobs in the universe. Theoretically, I could just sit and read my book until someone showed up wanting a buck's worth of gas. Practically, the Old Man would go nuts if he stopped in and found me with my nose in a book. In his view, there were always jobs that needed doing and I should seek them out.

The men's and ladies rooms were already nice and clean. I'd cleaned the office windows and scraped and swept up most of the crap from the shop floor. Short of restacking the oil cans, I was out of stupid make-work projects. The telephone saved me from climbing up in the parts loft to organize exhaust pipes.

It was Gail Ferguson, a girl from school. "Your mom said I could get you here," she sounded like she'd just run a mile. "Oh, Paddy, have you heard about Teddy?" she blurted, between gasps, "he crashed…and…" she was sobbing and couldn't continue.

"Teddy crashed his car? Tonight?"

"This afternoon sometime."

"What happened? Is Teddy okay? Where did they crash? How about Kevin and Larry, were they with him?"

Gail didn't answer for a minute. "The car flipped and went off the Island Bridge."

"My God, that's a drop of at least fifty feet and deep water. How badly are they hurt?"

"Kevin and Larry got out...Teddy was trapped in the car. Divers had to....Teddy's... dead, Paddy. That's all I know. You were friends so I thought you'd want to know...I'm sorry Paddy." And she hung up.

I didn't envy Teddy anymore.

Rowing to Ireland

"Row, fer crissakes!" Billy shouted at me. "We'll never get done at this rate."

I told him to shove it.

"Look, Paddy, you need to feather your oars, then take long, even strokes..." He stood up in the back of our skiff, put his hands over mine and, facing forward, rammed the oars into the stroke, then rolled our wrists to turn the edge of the blades to face the wind. "...like that."

"Jesus, man, you're going to break my wrists. You think a little wind resistance is going to make a difference?"

"I know it does – and I don't want to be out here all day while you figure it out."

"Aye, aye, Captain."

"Just row the damn boat, dummy."

I was getting rowing instruction in a boat reeking of rotting fish on a cold late-May morning because I had a hard time saying no to a friend. Billy and I had been sitting in the Greeks – a soda shop and convenience store that allowed us to read the magazines and put them back on the rack. The place even had a juke box that gave you six plays for a dime.

It was run by several generations of Armenian immigrants which some ignoramus had identified as "Greeks" – or maybe it was just easier to say. The first generation was in semi-retirement and the place was run by a second-generation son who didn't mind having teenagers hanging around the place. Billy and I and most of the kids from the neighborhood spent hours in the place smoking and reading the car magazines and lamenting the fact that the chance that any of us would ever own a cool car was just about zero.

The only times we were banned was during shift changes on the shipyard. The Greeks was just outside the shipyard's main gate and did a land office business at those times. Max, the first generation, would unplug the jukebox, grab the magazines out of our hands and shoo us out onto the pavement. An hour or so later, we'd go back, plug in the juke and pick up where we left off.

On the afternoon in question, Billy put down the current issue of *Car Craft* and laid out his great idea. "Paddy, my old man said the price of lobster is way up and people are putting their boats over earlier than ever this year. We could make a hell of a lot more fishing than working some shit job for minimum wage." Summer jobs were hard to come by in our home town – or were for sixteen-year-olds with leather jackets, greased back hair and hussy curls.

"How are we going to do that, man? We don't have a boat, traps, money for gas or bait…oh, and don't you have to have a license? On top of that, I don't know the first damned thing about lobstering."

Feeling that I'd properly demolished his suggestion, I went back to the review of the Ferrari Super America 400 in *Road and Track*. The reviewer thought the brakes were inadequate for the speed and power of the car – have to remember that when I'm in the market of a hundred-and fifty-thousand dollar car.

"I have a boat."

"Boat, hell," I laughed, "you have a leaky skiff that your old man uses to get out to the moorings."

"It floats. I can get some old pots on the cheap that we can fix." He paused, obviously waiting for me to object. When I didn't, he finished with, "...and I have a license."

"No shit?"

"No shit."

The minimum age for a license was sixteen, but only a limited number were issued, which made them expensive and hard to get. Billy had apparently swung it somehow. Much later, I discovered that it was his father's license. Billy had just taken advantage of being William Nelson *Junior*, figuring he could bluff his way out of any inspection. His name *was* William Nelson, after all.

So we spent the next week repairing the old, busted-up traps that Billy got for us – hell, some of them were so old that they still had the curved willow branches as ribs. His sister, Angela, knew how to knit heads, the net-like structures inside the trap that actually did the trapping, and let us owe her for the ones we needed. With eight traps and buoys, a little bait ("borrowed" from the lobsterman next door) we were ready to launch our business. We had agreed beforehand that whatever we made would be divided by three, a share each for Billy, me and one for the boat. Heck, he had the license and the boat – how could I argue?

At first we set our pots in the shallow water of the back channel, venturing only a little way into the river. The river itself, actually a tidal estuary, shelved off quickly to deep water and had a wicked four to six knot current. It was no place for a small boat. We didn't have enough rope (called warp) anyway – and probably couldn't get the traps off the bottom if we did. I never did find out how much a foot of wet lobster warp weighs. Hauling a hundred feet nearly killed me. Hauling two-hundred feet by hand against the current was probably impossible.

Our little business got off to a decent start although I had a few hard facts to learn. I learned that pulling a twenty-pound lobster trap with a hundred feet of wet warp to the surface by hand was damned hard work. Working boats used a winch to haul their traps. The lobsterman just snagged the buoy, wrapped a couple of turns of warp around the pulley, and engaged the winch. It did the heavy work while he just coiled the warp.

Our little boat didn't have room for a winch, even if we could have afforded one. We hauled them the old-fashioned way, hand-over-hand.

My second dose of reality was that most of the time there would be nothing in the trap when I got it to the surface. More than half the time, all we did is drag the trap up onto the gunwale, bait it, and heave it back overboard. This led inescapably to a third fact, make sure that the warp wasn't coiled around your ankle before the trap went overboard.

Even having lobsters in the trap didn't guaranty that you had anything to sell – they had to meet the rule. A legal lobster had to be at least 3¼ inches but not more than 5 inches from the eye socket to the back of the shell. The little ones needed to be allowed to grow and the big ones were the primary procreators. The legal arbiter of a trapped lobster's fate was a brass rule with a tooth at one end and the legal range etched along the stem. The tooth was hooked into the lobster's eye socket and the rule would immediately determine if it was legal. There's nothing quite as frustrating as straining your already-aching back and shoulder muscles to haul a trap, see three lobsters (and dollar signs) in it, and watch Billy throw all three back because they didn't meet the damn brass rule.

After I got used to the labor and developed some calluses, our little business looked like it could be a winner. Most afternoons we'd get four or five legal lobsters and head over to sell them.

We sold our catch to the Overlook Lobster House, a big restaurant on a pier over the river that catered to summer tourists. The management liked the patrons to see the chef in his white coat standing on the float negotiating for lobsters with fishermen. Can't get much fresher than that, the tourists figured. No one told the tourists that what they saw wasn't a tenth of the supply the Overlook needed or that the rest was brought in by trucks like every other restaurant. It was the image that people took back to Boston, or New York, or Omaha that mattered. Local boys hawking fresh lobsters. How quaint, the real New England.

It didn't take us long to realize that some pots were producing far more than others. Relocation was the obvious answer.

I offered the obvious solution. "Billy, we need to move some of these traps. Maybe, closer to those two at the end of Navy Island. Those are our best locations."

"You mean we need to find more spots in between the thirty other traps that are already there? Maybe get our asses kicked or get tossed overboard?" Billy lit a cigarette and contemplated my foolishness, "Don't you remember the shit we took the first time?"

When we set our first traps in that area, we got yelled at and threatened. I never did find out exactly how close you could set your pot to some other fisherman's – it appeared to depend on shouted negotiations involving threats to cut the offending trap's warp, sinking your boat, and beating the bejesus out of you. Billy was good at the negotiating and got the others to accept two of our pots right where the back channel and the main channel connected. Our traps sat on an underwater shelf only about fifty feet down and less than twenty yards from the island that housed the town's big shipyard.

"Maybe we could find a spot. It's worth a try isn't it?" I tried a little flattery, "you managed to get us two spots, why not two more – might have to be a little further out in the river, but who cares?"

We were allowed to set two more traps a little farther out into the river in deeper water, but still possible to fish by hand. The first time we hauled them, we got six legal lobsters. Maybe that Ferrari was in my future after all.

Then the damn motor quit.

Almost at the end of our string of traps, it just stopped.

"Check the gas," Billy ordered as we drifted.

"How damn dumb do you think I am?" I had fueled that beast before we left. But I checked to be sure. "This piece of crap is almost as bad as a Mercury – we were as brand conscious about outboard motors as about cars in those days.

"Probably some rust or other hundred-year-old crud plugged the gas line or the carb." I yanked the starter rope about twenty times, getting more furious by the pull. It didn't even fire.

Drifting with the current further from our last two pots, I was ready to head for shore and quit the whole deal – and maybe a little scared. "Okay, genius," I asked with poisoned politeness, "now what the hell do we do? Just drift until we bump into a pier somewhere. Without your shitty little motor, we don't even have a way to get home."

"Don't get your knickers in a twist, Paddy. We just have to row for a few days until we get the motor running again."

"Row?" I couldn't believe him. "Row? All the way from your old man's dock down the channel and back? Are you nuts?"

"Are you some kind of sissy, or what?" Billy sneered. "It won't be that hard."

It was my ineptitude as a rower that caused Billy's exasperation. After getting bitched out, I slowed and deepened my strokes and started feathering the oars as I rowed to the last two pots in our eight-pot string. I had to admit that the boat moved more smoothly and easily through the water with less effort – maybe Billy was on to something. Prior to joining Billy in a lobster-fishing enterprise, the only rowing I'd done was on the small lake where my family had a cottage – and then only when I didn't have money to put gas in the motor boat. The weak, sloppy way I handled the oars was adequate there, but pretty clearly not up to the demands of the wind and waves of the harbor. It had never crossed my mind that anyone would rely on this primitive form of propulsion to actually get anywhere – it was as outlandish as trying to haul our traps in a birchbark canoe.

That was the beginning of our adventure in lobstering the way our Colonial ancestors did it. After rowing around to haul our traps and sell what we caught, we'd go back to the boatyard and try to get the motor running.

My back was killing me as I pulled on the oars (feathering each stroke) from our last trap to the Overlook. "This stinks, man. We have to get that crappy motor running," I groused.

"Don't be dumb," Billy laughed, "the damn tourists love it. Remember yesterday when they came down to take pictures? We probably ought to just buy some lobsters and row 'em over there to sell 'em."

We both laughed at the ignorance and gullibility of tourists – without thinking too hard about who was busting their back fishing and who was eating the lobsters.

After days of working on the motor, we concluded that the magneto, the thing that generates the spark to fire the gas, had crapped out. And, unlike a car generator which sits out nicely where you can get at it, an outboard's magneto is attached to the end of the crankshaft under the flywheel.

"Well, Paddy, this looks like where you earn your keep." Billy tossed all of the responsibility into my lap.

"I haven't been earning my keep up 'til now? You can kiss my ass."

My hurt feelings notwithstanding, we had to get the motor running and I did have more mechanical skill than Billy.

After removing the recoil starter and the fuel tank – and splashing gas all over myself – I was faced with figuring out how to pull the flywheel and get at the magneto.

As I was pondering, Billy's older brother, Hank, wandered by.

"You guys using that old motor?" he asked. "It's got a bad magneto, you know. Keeps cutting out."

"Gee, thanks, Hank."

"Yeah, and a new one would cost as much as a new motor. You guys are just wasting your time on that piece of junk."

"Okay, Bill, we need to find a used motor somewhere. How much money's in the boat fund?"

"What do you mean? What boat fund?"

"This is coming out of the boat's share, right?" I demanded.

His red face told me everything. "You already spent it?"

"Well…"

We were doomed to row from pot to pot until we could earn enough to buy a motor – and get my half of what Billy already spent. At least, my rowing form was now up to his standards.

Two days later we went on our ocean adventure. We were hauling the new traps at the end of Navy Island while the tide was in full ebb. It was my turn to row while Billy hauled up the pot, but we were in deep water and it took both of us to get the damn thing off the bottom. Billy took over while I started rowing us back to where we'd return the trap after Billy had gotten out the lobsters and baited it.

That's when my heart jumped into my throat. When I realized that we were at least half a mile from the end of the island and moving out into the harbor...fast. I started rowing like crazy – with good form – trying to pull us back to the shelter of the island. No matter how hard I pulled, we kept heading out. Shit!

The laws of the physical universe seemed to have changed – I knew I was making progress, I could see the wake the boat was leaving, but instead of slowly unrolling behind us, the shore kept racing by going the wrong way! I couldn't figure it out...

"Hey, look, we got four in this one trap," Billy exclaimed, oblivious of our predicament. "That makes eleven today! We'll be able to get the motor fixed pretty quick." Then he looked around. "Where the hell..."

Then it hit me what was happening. "OH MY GOD! BILLY, WE'RE IN THE CURRENT!" I was making half a knot toward shore across the surface of the water while the water itself was heading out to sea at seven knots! We were on a really long, fast treadmill and couldn't possibly keep up.

"C'mon, dummy, you'll never get anywhere rowing against the current. Turn the boat and row with it. Angle across it toward Dog Island while I get this secured." He got the trap all the way into the boat, then helped me row as hard as we could toward the little island at the mouth of the harbor.

It soon became clear that we weren't going to make it. "Let me get these oilskins and boots off, I'm going to swim for it," I yelled.

"Don't be a frigging idiot," Billy barked and shoved me back onto the seat. "You won't be able to swim against the tide any more than you could row against it. And, the water's so cold you'd just go numb and drown." He opened the trap and started pulling out, measuring and pegging the four lobsters. He put them in the basket. "Help me get this overboard before we swamp!" I noticed that he broke the door off the trap and threw it over separately. He was a fisherman to the end – didn't want lobsters to get stuck in the trap and never be able to get out. He was worried about the damn lobsters! Shit! The way things were going we might be having a face to face conversation down there soon.

We missed Dog Island by less than fifty yards and were soon bobbing in big swells that hinted at the actual Atlantic. We were facing big, green rollers, four or five feet from trough to crest in a dinky little twelve-foot boat. Unbidden a phrase from the seaman's prayer popped into my head "Oh, Lord, your sea is so vast and my boat so small…"

I knew enough to quarter the waves – crossing them at an angle to avoid either plowing straight into them or turning sideways. The skiff didn't have the tall bow and foredeck of blue-water boats that allowed them to breast the waves without taking on water. If we made a mistake and dug into a wave, we'd be driven straight to the bottom.

At the same time, I had to fight to keep the boat from its tendency to turn broadside to the waves, which would either capsize us or bring tons of water over the gunwale, again pushing our little boat straight down.

Billy had come aft and was helping me row much as he did during my lesson, pushing forward while I pulled back. It also put more weight toward the stern raising the bow and giving us a little margin of error if we went into a wave too sharply. Since he was facing forward, he could also guide us better than I had been able to.

All we could do was row into the waves at an angle, ride them up, then skate down the back side into the trough trying not to broach. Billy was yelling, "starboard oar! Starboard!" as the boat started to turn left, then "both together!" as we pulled through the trough and up the face of the next wave. I was sure that each wave was going to be our last. If the waves in the outer harbor were giving us this much trouble, what were we going to do when the current took us all the way out to sea? I'd pretty much given up hope but kept on rowing – we were going to drown, but I wasn't going down without a fight.

Billy suddenly stood up on the thwart – what the hell? Is suicide his only alternative? Hell, I thought I'd be the one who snapped. I grabbed his arm to keep him from going overboard. He was madly waving his other arm in the air.

"He's seen us!" he shouted as he flopped down. "Jesus, don't swamp us now," as he pointed at the oncoming wall of cold, green water.

At the crest of the next wave, I could see a lobster boat chugging steadily toward us. It even looked familiar – I had an instant of fear that I was hallucinating. The seasick-green cabin roof and bright orange rails looked like Gus Brouchard's Tina Marie. We saw her every day when we tied up at the Overlook. If we could stay above water for a little while longer, we'd be saved.

Gus pulled up on our weather side, putting us in the lee of the Tina Marie and giving us some shelter. "Looks like you're in a little trouble, Billy. Need help?"

"Naw, Gus," said Billy, "we were planning to row to Ireland. Are we headed in the right direction?"

"Ayuh. Can't be more than twenty-five-hundred miles. Whyn't you blue water sailors heave me a line and I'll tow you in."

We clambered aboard the Tina Marie and tied our skiff off against a stern cleat. After making sure that the skiff was riding safely in the wake of the lobster boat, Gus asked "what the fuck were you two knotheads doing? I see lobster'n gear, but you got no business out this far. Christ, Billy, you don't even have a motor on that death trap!" He noted our basket and got the same look in his eye that I've seen in farmers and fishermen my whole life.

"Ya know, boys, I'm gonna hafta go outta my way to get you back home. My little Buick uses plenty of fuel on a side trip like that." His little Buick was a four-hundred-fifty-four cubic inch V-8 that could push the Tina Marie at more than thirty miles an hour. Gus liked his boats to be fast. "Don't suppose ya got any money for gas, do ya?"

"If we had any money, would we be rowing out here?"

"Wahl, I wasna talkin about that kind of money – just a few dollars for fuel, ya know."

"Nope, we're broke."

"Then ya won't mind if I just take you back to my dock and let ya row from there, okay?"

"Tell you what, Gus," Billy began, "we've got a couple of legal lobsters that we could give you to help cover the fuel costs. How do you feel about that?"

"I'm using a lot of fuel, what with towing your boat and going out of my way and all. How many lobsters ya got anyway?"

"Six and we'll split 'em with you."

"I believe all six would be fair. Remember, if it weren't for me, you'd still be out there or drownded."

"Give up, Billy," I pleaded, "I don't want to row any farther."

"Okay, our six lobsters and you deliver us to my father's dock." Gus probably knew that there were more than the six Billy admitted to but he'd gotten a good deal. The six lobsters would bring him maybe fifteen dollars and even the Tina Marie wouldn't suck up more than a couple of gallons making the detour. At thirty-five cents a gallon, say a dollar's worth, Gus's humanitarian endeavor would show a tidy profit. I didn't care, I would have given him a medal – and Billy's damn boat.

After Gus delivered us to the Nelson's float and helped us get the skiff in, we settled up. "Pretty sharp, boy," was Gus's only comment when Billy handed over the six lobsters and clearly had almost as many still in the basket. Then he chuckled, "Woulda done for nothin'" With a roar, the Tina Marie pulled away from the dock and headed down the channel to home.

Billy's father was standing up on the dock. "We put in a new mooring while you were out skylarking around," he rumbled. "Used that piece of shit motor you've been tinkering with as part of the anchor. Thought you'd want to know."

Thus Billy and Paddy's Lobster Company disappeared beneath the waves figuratively rather than actually. We didn't drown and I learned something – don't quit, the Tina Marie might be just over the horizon...And, of course, I also learned how to row.

To this day, when the thought of having a big sailboat that could take me cruising on blue water comes over me, the memory of those huge, uncaring waves rolling toward Billy and me in that little boat is enough to banish it.

Mrs. Hastings

As befits the original and, for a hundred years, the only building of the Academy – the private school serving as my home town's public high school, the Main Building had its own atmosphere. Walking through the doors, you were met with the smell of generations of chalk dust and hormones, of frustration and enlightenment in keeping with nearly a hundred years of serving teenagers. During the baby boom, however, Main's three uncompromising brick stories were joined by several undistinguished and sterile modern structures.

I expect that it will eventually be replaced by an insipid low-rise box with air conditioning. Its razing will undoubtedly be justified by claims of greater energy efficiency, better student experiences, and the inevitable invasion of computers. Tradition be damned!

When I attended, there were obvious paths worn into the hardwood floors by generations of students. Every night, the janitor waxed and buffed those floors, scenting the morning classes with the bees wax applied the night before.

Back then, the top floor, the domain of the English department, was mostly staffed by women who apparently came with the building. As a group, they were frighteningly well-educated and seemed to belong to a different species from us.

Occasionally, one lamented the error of eliminating Greek as a parallel foundation with Latin for truly understanding English. All of my high school English instruction took place on that floor. Teachers' directions whispered down the corridors and through time, having changed little from a hundred years ago, leaving verbal trail marks to guide the generations,"...now, class, conjugate the verb to be" and, "...what is Stephen Crane telling us?" And, of course, the dim mumblings of the poor students trying to answer.

I loved the timelessness of the building – knowing that we could be sitting at the same desks as our great-grandfathers – and wrestling with the same texts. Unfortunately, my love had more to do with the romance of an old building than a commitment to scholarship. It is no wonder that my slap-dash effort and impudent attitude led to frequent confrontations with the deities of the top floor – most often with Mrs. Hastings.

"Mr. Meecham, would you be so kind as to come up front and read your...essay?... on the book *Way of a Wanton* by Richard S. Prather?"

I was hoping that the glint in her eye was a mischievous twinkle, not the glare of a vengeful goddess. "Since it's a little outside our normal reading list, you might want to provide your classmates with some background first. Tell us just who this Mr. Prather is... his claim to fame...rank in literature?"

Oh my God! She was actually going to make me read what I had written.

The assignment had been to analyze the motivations and internal conflicts of the main characters in a book of our choosing. The book I chose was a pulp detective story, full of violence and as much sex and foul language as could be printed in books sold over the counter. Its cover was graced by a voluptuous woman in a slinky evening dress looking back over her shoulder at the reader. She would have been right at home on the nose of a B-17 heading for Nazi Germany. In addition to being my most recent reading, I had picked it, as much as anything, to tweak Mrs. Hastings. After all, she did say a book of our own choosing.

Judith Carrington had already bored us with ten minutes on *Uncle Tom's Cabin*. "...Topsy had internalized the systemic racism that existed alongside the overt subjugation evident in the slave-holding South..." And on and on.

Judith was smart and her liberal sympathies fueled a powerful flame of commitment to the Civil Rights struggle. It wouldn't have hurt me to listen – except that the whole issue seemed irrelevant. After all, there were no imported minorities in town – we were lily-white and forced to discriminate against each other. Hell, until I left grammar school, I thought Jews were an extinct race, like Abyssinians or Sumerians.

Next up had been Ramona Latham who talked about the inner struggles of Tess D'Urbervilles while the struggle inside of Ramona's blouse kept me interested. Then Ronny Jacobs who probably hadn't even completed reading the Cliff Notes – there was some doubt in my mind if he could read at all – stuttered and stammered describing the horrors witnessed by Gordon Pym in Edgar Allen Poe's novel recording Pym's fictional journey. Shifting from foot-to-foot, he concluded that the book wasn't very realistic.

Then Mrs. Hastings had called on me.

"Ah, are you sure you want me to read?" I panicked because the character on whom I'd lavished my lascivious attention was a "chesty Polish girl, named Wanda...with legs up to her neck" I had attributed to her deep internal conflicts between her religious upbringing and her line of work – prostitution.

61

"Yes, Mr. Meecham, I think we all would benefit from your insights."

"The Way of a Wanton, by Richard S. Prather" I began. I had started the piece with a quote from the book that would probably get me expelled, "...she was a big girl, almost six feet in a short skirt that emphasized the swing of her hips and long silk-clad legs. A tight sweater, heavy blonde mane, red lips and nails like daggers completed her work clothes."

The class tittered, the girls covering their mouths and the boys grinning at each other. I could feel the heat of terminal embarrassment rising in my face. I hesitated, hoping that Mrs. Hastings would rescue me.

"Mr. Meecham," she said....

Thank God, she's going to grant my prayer.

"As I said earlier, I think it would be well for you to tell us a little about the narrator before you continue."

"The, ah, narrator?"

"Yes, who said she was a big girl with swinging hips et cetera? The book is written in the first person, is it not?"

"Um..."

"I'll make it easier. The story is told from a particular point of view. Whose?"

"The detective, Shell Scott," I answered.

"Tell us about Mr. Scott. His background, his goals, his...desires?"

"He's a private detective that ..."

"Who"

"Huh?"

"He's a private detective *who* does something."

Sweat dripped down my forehead forcing me to blink and wipe my stinging eyes. "The detective, Shell Scott helps people in trouble *who* can't get help from the police. He drinks and often finds himself involved with beautiful women."

Mrs. Hasting grilled me in front of the class for twenty minutes eliciting laughter, embarrassment, and shock from the class until the bell finally released me.

As I scurried my way out the door, she handed me my paper with an "A" on it. "Good writing." Looking straight into my eyes, she continued, "Don't do it again."

Those were the days when teachers really were grossly underpaid and, in New England, subject to a strict code of conduct enforced by an army of peeping busybodies. Mrs. Hastings had to have a true calling to put up with it – and us. She was not young, was new in our school, and was rumored to be divorced. At least, there was no father at home for her daughter who was in class with us.

I was the indulged first-born son in my family. We didn't have much, but whatever we did have, I always got more than my sisters. Thoughtlessly accepting my privileged position, I drifted through life. I was, after all, special. School came easily. I was always in the top group, always got the best grades, always smiled upon by teachers. I took it as my due.

Until Mrs. Hastings punctured my self-important balloon.

After *The Way of a Wanton* massacre, she even had the courage to take me on as a project. She pushed and pushed to get me to extend myself. "What did you really see? Show me the quote that supports your statement. You're reading Pablum – challenge yourself." Her hectoring was never-ending but so subtly done that the rest of the class never saw it.

I was so desperate that I even considered asking her tall, quiet, cat-eyed daughter out on a date figuring that she might put in a good word for me. Of course, my track record with girls suggested that – even if she agreed to go out with me – her good judgment might later encourage her toward increasing my punishment rather than reducing it. I discarded the date strategy as too risky.

So it continued for two years, both junior and senior English. I rarely escaped from her class without an extra assignment or a piece from a literary journal. When other kids asked me to intercede with Mrs. Hastings for them, I really started to worry that I was considered "teacher's pet." But I kept doing the assignments and reading the articles anyway.

She was the advisor for the school's student correspondent to the local newspaper – namely, me – and required a weekly Friday afternoon review of what I was working on for my monthly story. One time my offering was particularly thin, consisting primarily of sports scores.

"Aren't you ashamed of this," she chastised waving my two dog-eared pages. "It's the work – or non-work – of an exceptionally lazy young man who takes nothing very seriously."

I hung my head, waiting for her to be done.

"Don't you realize that even something as trivial as this is *read* by people? You have *readers*! You owe them more effort than you're putting in."

"If you want me to quit, I will," I mumbled. "Didn't want the job anyway."

"Oh, no, you don't get to quit, Mr. Meecham. You have the ability and you owe it to yourself to use it. Laziness is a betrayal of your potential."

"Why are you doing this to me?" I whined.

"By that, I assume you mean encouraging you to actually work. My answer is that I am not doing anything *to* you – I am doing it *for* you."

"Well, what do you want?"

"If you must have specific assignments, I'll give you one. By next Friday, bring me five hundred words on the student viewpoint on the space race – especially from the standpoint of competing resources."

I wasn't completely sure what she meant by "competing resources" but I would have nodded yes to anything to get out of that room. I gathered up my books and headed for the door.

Her voice stopped me before I managed my escape.

"Remember, eight o'clock tomorrow in Mrs. Silver's room," she said.

"Huh?" Had she slipped yet another assignment onto my list while I wasn't paying attention?

"Tomorrow morning, Mr. Meecham. Certainly you remember The National Merit test? I'm proctoring, but it's in Mrs. Silver's room. It's a little larger than this one."

"Um...what test is that?"

"Are you telling me that you aren't signed up for the test?" If anything, she was more exasperated with me than when she carved up my newspaper story. She dug in her desk drawer, pulled out some papers, and slapped the package down in front of me. "Fill that out. As proctor I can register you late."

She watched while I filled out the forms, then reviewed them to be sure I'd done it correctly. "Very well, be in Mrs. Silver's room at eight with several number two pencils and fifteen dollars."

"Ah, fifteen dollars? I don't know if..."

Bob McCrillis

"Be there at eight."

Of course I showed up … without the money. The Old Man didn't get home with his pay until really late, and I was afraid to wake him before I left for school. My mother didn't have fifteen dollars, "I have to get something for lunch today with the little bit I have," Ma said. "Can't you owe them?"

At ten minutes to eight, we were all lined up to get our test booklets from Mrs. Hastings. I managed to be at the end of the line. Each kid handed her fifteen dollars – mostly in cash – which she deposited in an official-looking envelope on her desk. "At least one desk between each of you in each direction," she instructed, then turned to me. "Mr. Meecham, you made it. I'm glad to see you!"

"I'm sorry, Mrs. Hastings, I don't have the money. My father got home late and…"

Her eyes narrowed. "Oh," she said and, after a brief hesitation, brusquely checked off my name and handed me my booklet. "Find a seat."

Since the only desks available were in the first row. I had an excellent vantage point to watch her dig into her purse and put money into the envelope.

It took three days of whining at home for me to get the money, but on Wednesday, I was able to meet my obligation to my teacher. That lessened the humiliation a little.

About a month later, Mrs. Hastings strolled into study hall and dropped an envelope on my desk. "Looks like you'll have your choice of colleges, Patrick," she smiled. "Good work."

Everyone watched while I opened the envelope. My test results were the third highest in the state. Colleges from across the country recruited me and offered financial aid packages that made it possible for me to attend.

Mrs. Hastings

I did attend college on an almost free ride, wasted much of the opportunity, and followed my father and grandfather into the Marine Corps, eventually to Viet Nam. It wasn't until I was back in the world that I realized that my degree, however reluctantly obtained or deserved, gave me choices that most of the guys didn't have. All because of Mrs. Hastings.

I'm ashamed that I never had the good manners to thank her.

Inspiration

The Queen

I was bored. It was raining and there was nothing on television – wouldn't have mattered anyway because my grandmother was watching some preacher promise a life of wonders for anyone with a couple of extra dollars to send him.

My sisters and I were on our monthly visit to Gram. When my grandfather was alive, the three of us usually trailed after him like baby ducks after their mama while he fixed things or painted things or just walked around the old farmstead. After his death, Ma and my Old Man said we should keep the visits up so the Gram didn't get too lonely. She spent a good bit of her time watching television and knitting, but was usually good for a card game or two in the afternoon. She played gin, poker and a game called reno – and she played for blood. After she'd taken all our matchsticks, she'd retire to the kitchen to make dinner or the living room to watch television, and we were on our own.

At thirteen, I wanted no part of my sisters, I'd finished my book, Gram was being proselytized and it was too wet and cold to go outside so I retreated to the attic. The attic was my secret daydreaming place, a single huge slanted-ceiling room filled with mysterious boxes, chests, furniture and dust. It was also a place where I could hide from my sisters – they said it was "creepy." Climbing the steep curving stairs with the leprechaun-size treads, I entered King Tut's tomb or a Pueblo Kiva or a golden cave under the Queen Maeve's mound. Or, sometimes it was just a log cabin in the woods miles from civilization and yards from hostile tribes.

The thin, grey light from the tiny windows at the gable ends caught the floating dust motes and the silent dress dummies and cast a glamour over the space. I felt that it was in a place between worlds. I happily rooted among the treasures of past times until something struck a spark off the steel of my imagination and I was off on a new journey. Some distant relative's uniform from the Great War would transport me to the trenches in Flanders where I avoided poison gas and machine gun fire while racing across no-man's land to engage the Kaiser's minions, or maybe chasing Pancho Villa with Black Jack Pershing.

My happiest discoveries were the photographs and old newspapers – I could readily insert myself as the hero in adventures I knew about, but these items showed me adventures of which I'd been unaware. A dozen dinky black and white photos of people in antique clothing posing with a Model-T Ford led me to my mother's story of her grandfather driving across the country in that Ford. She didn't remember why it was necessary, only that her grandmother and grandfather, along with several relatives drove from Massachusetts to California and back shortly after the turn of the century. Some of the newspapers in that same carton advertised farm tractors that were apparently small steam locomotives with studded steel wheels and, for the ladies, whalebone corsets. I can't remember which idea seemed crazier to me.

When I was little, I used to drape one of the dress dummies in some of the old clothes, put a scary mask on its face, and stand it at the head of the stairs to make sure my sisters didn't defile the space. As we got older, I became committed and they lost interest so the dress dummy went back to being naked.

The door to the attic stairs was always kept locked – which added just a whiff of the forbidden. To get up there, I had to get the key from the board in the kitchen, climb the back stairs, and unlock a door in the hall. (I would have locked it behind me if I wasn't afraid I wouldn't be able to get it unlocked again). At the top of the stairs I was directly under the peak of the roof fifteen feet above me.

Heavy timbers mated to each other marched away from me in both directions supporting the roof and, in turn, supported by huge wooden posts every ten or twelve feet. The massive construction confidently stated "I'm here forever." Standing there, I had a sense of obdurate, unshakable endurance, unaffected by fashion or the whims of the people passing through. The attic's majesty was tempered by the human touches of an encyclopedia of household and farm items, dangling from wooden pegs and nails, that decorated the beams. The posts also served as canvasses for the graffiti of multiple generations of Carters – some in pencil, some carved with a jackknife, some painted. I'd often enjoyed making up stories about the more cryptic notes. Did MC and JS ever marry? Who was

"Freyer" and in what code was *13W oak 117 2/3 Fryer*? The beams contained evidence of many transient passersby and the homely marks of their passage.

On this particular day, I rediscovered the treasure chest that had gotten me a painful spanking. It was a small leather-skinned case shaped like a steamer trunk, but only about a quarter the size. It looked like the strongboxes featured in many of the westerns I devoured. The last time I'd seen it was years ago – I think I was eight – right after my grandfather died.

At that time, the chest had been lying open on my grandmother's bed. There were some papers and such spread out around it. At eight years old and inquisitive – a nice word for nosy – I couldn't resist peeking. The first thing that caught my eye was a photograph on the front page of a yellowed copy of the *Boston Clarion* from June 5, 1928. The picture showed a man in a suit lying face down on the ground with blood running from underneath him down towards the gutter. A uniformed state trooper holding a Thompson submachine gun like a trophy stood over the body smiling for the camera. The caption explained that Trooper Warren Richards displayed the weapon of choice recovered from Meecham's body.

"Meecham?" that's my name. Could this be some relation of ours? I might be related to a gangster? Cool! I moved closer and looked into the chest.

"What do you think you're doing?" my grandmother's voice was like a nail driven into my eight-year-old skull. "How dare you poke around in my things!" she screeched. "Get out, get out now!"

The Queen

"But, Gram, this guy has the same..."

She grabbed me by the hair and frog-marched me out to the living room, shoved me into a chair, and ordered me to, "stay put. I'll deal with you in a minute."

Both Mary and Alice stared at me with open anticipation of witnessing a gruesome punishment for whatever sin I'd committed.

Gram came back with a belt. "Stand up," she barked. "Lean over the table."

"I didn't mean any...."

Whack! The leather belt sent a jolt of pain all the way to the top of my head. Whack! Whack! Whack! My grandmother was a big, strong woman – I expected to be permanently crippled. Whack! Whack!

"I'll teach you to stick your nose where it doesn't belong." Whack! "Nosy little boys who..." Whack! "can't..." Whack! "mind..." Whack! "their own..." Whack! "business." Whack, whack, whack! "Now go to your room and stay there until I call you."

The clear message from my younger self to my thirteen-year-old self was, don't mess with that little chest – the next time she would drive home the fear of God or introduce me to Him immediately.

Did I listen to that eight-year-old voice ? Of course not – I wasn't a little boy anymore and I wasn't afraid of my grandmother (she'd never catch me now anyhow). Just one little look to find out who the dead gangster was. That's all I wanted – just one little look. No one would ever know.

This time it was the handbill that got me rather than the newspaper. Right on top. It crackled with age as I unrolled it releasing a puff of ancient dust near my nose. Opened, it revealed a line drawing a woman holding an old-fashioned microphone stand with one hand while reaching for an angel or a star outside and above the frame. Her fringed flapper-style shift fit closely enough in a few places to hint at the shapely woman inside. Her piratical head band, double string of waist-length beads and extreme makeup evoked the Charleston, bathtub gin, and Prohibition.

It wasn't the drawing that froze me in mid-thought – it was the name. Sweeping across the dusky pink spotlight in script was *Rae Carter*. The handbill promised fine dining and entertainment by the "highly-acclaimed songstress" at Farrel's Place in Rochester. Rae Carter? My grandmother?

I studied the face. It was only a drawing and probably somewhat generic, but the planes of the face, deep-set dark eyes and full lips could be her...

Not possible! My teetotaling, Christian Scientist grandmother singing in a speakeasy? That seemed no more likely than a flock of flying pigs. I put the handbill aside and dug deeper into the chest.

Under the handbill, yellowed newspapers crumbled with age and shedding dust made up the top layer. On the very top was the *Boston Clarion* that I'd seen before. The headline over the photograph that had caused me so much pain read

"3 Gangsters Killed in Lightning Raid." Acting on a tip, a combined force of state and local police raided an isolated farmhouse in Donnerville reported to be the hideout of a gang of robbers that had terrorized northeastern Massachusetts and New Hampshire for more than six months. When they approached the farmhouse, the law officers were met with a hail of gunfire. In the ensuing gunfight three of the robbers were killed and two more were captured along with two women. One of the men killed was one Edward L. "Eddie" Meecham, known for his use of a machine gun in his robberies."

I had heard the name Eddie Meecham mentioned at family gatherings. When I asked my Old Man about him, he growled, "Eddie Meecham was my father. That son of a bitch." Then he glared at me, "satisfied now?"

In the same way that we all have a sick need to look at a car crash when we drive by, I had to keep poking at the "Eddie Meecham" mystery. My mother simply offered that "Gram's first husband was a bad man who left her flat after your father was born. Of course, that was a long time ago – she's put all that behind her now."

Now, here among the many mysteries, I had the chance to resolve one. The archives were there. All I had to do was overcome my fear of Gram's fury. Of course, I was much sneakier now. I quietly crept back down the attic stairs and locked the hall door. When I returned to the treasure chest, I removed and read the old newspapers following story of the bank robbers, taking care not to further damage the pages.

I learned that New Hampshire was one of the few states that had a policy of non-extradition – the state would not send wanted criminals back to the states where the crimes were committed. As long as there was no crime in New Hampshire, there would be no trouble with the law. This made it a haven for criminals wanted in other states – an idiosyncratic policy for an idiosyncratic state. The Meecham gang all came from the Detroit area and had moved from bootlegging to bank robbery, which multiplied the pressure on the group from law enforcement so much that they sought a temporary respite in New Hampshire. The well-fixed and free-spending gangsters were generally popular with the stony-broke locals especially among the young local women whose choices prior to the arrival of the Detroit faction were decidedly dull.

The Manchester paper reported that the group had been slipping across the border to plunder Massachusetts institutions and replenish their coffers. Once the gang unknowingly made the mistake of robbing a bank inside the state, the full wrath of their host was brought down on them.

The role of the two women captured in the cabin was "uncertain." The story went on to disclose that one of the women was a noted local singer, Rae Carter. Gram!

My church-lady grandmother was a gun moll? Too cool! This would definitely top Billy's brother's trip to the County Jail in our leather jacket and Brylcreem set. I was the descendent of a real criminal right out of the gangster movies – hell, Meecham even used a Tommy gun! But, of course, I couldn't talk to Gram about it.

For two more visits I stealthily plundered the treasure chest. A scrapbook with photos of a woman – I assume Gram – on stage, marked-up sheet music for *Always* by Irving Berlin, reviews – not all good – came to the surface. At the bottom of the chest were two cocktail dresses carefully folded in tissue, a silver flask with garter, a matching cigarette case and, lying among all the dainty silken things, a .45 caliber revolver. There were spent shells in all six chambers of the .45 and no extra ammunition.

The last thing I rifled was a sealskin document pouch containing a birth certificate for George Howard Meecham, my father, a probation certificate for Rae Lee Carter dated 9/20/1928, and a discharge and release from probation for Rae Lee Carter dated 12/30/1929. There was no marriage certificate or anything indicating that Eddie Meecham and Rae Carter had ever formalized their relationship. Could that be what my grandmother was hiding? Something as common as an illegitimate birth? That was so old-fashioned – nobody bothers about that now.

I carefully replaced everything in the chest and returned it to where I found it. I'd gotten my answers. My grandmother had been a wild one when she was younger – maybe wilder than many. She sure wasn't a whole lot of fun now – it was almost as if the exploits of Rae Carter involved some other woman.

I pondered how one person could be so different – do other old people have things like this hidden away. The possibilities flooded my brain.

"Well, Paddy, are you done snooping?" My grandmother's voice was as cold and hard as a granite gravestone.

I couldn't breathe, my pulse was hammering, and I wanted to run but was paralyzed.

"Well?" she glared at me, her hawk-like visage never harder or more intimidating.

"Ah, what?" I felt like a rabbit noticing the hawk's shadow had grown suddenly larger.

"Snooping, prying into things that don't concern you, going through other people private treasures. Are you done?"

"Gram, I wasn't snooping…it's just that I wanted to know…"

"You wanted to know things about me that you have no business knowing." Her eyes, always very dark brown, now were black with no whites at all. With her blade-like nose, high cheekbones and dark, yellow-brown skin, she could double as an Aztec Queen ready to send a sacrifice to his death.

"Isn't that the truth, Patrick? You snuck up to the attic and rummaged through my case just to satisfy your own meddling curiosity and thought I wouldn't find out" She turned and headed back down the stairs. "You come with me and bring my case."

She sat me down at the yellow Formica table in her kitchen – the scene of so many take-no-prisoners gin games and comfort food dinners – then sat beside me with the chest on the table in front of us. It was just the two of us – she must have sent Mary and Alice on an errand or something.

While she opened the chest, I tried to weasel my way out of trouble, "Gram, the things you did were cool. After I saw the picture in the newspaper…"

"So you think that a photograph of the man I loved lying dead in the dirt is cool? You think I enjoy thinking about it? Did you ever even think about me?"

"Well, no. I didn't think about it that way," I stammered.

"Of course you didn't think of it that way – you're a little kid. Well you're going to grow up a little right now, Sonny Jim."

She couldn't whip me with a belt anymore. What was her plan? She lifted the handbill out and unrolled it. Lost in reverie, she said quietly, "Eddie Meecham gave me a better life, and I loved him for it." Turning to me her anger returned, "but that didn't matter to you, did it?"

"What did I…"

"Shut your mouth and listen. I'm going to tell you a story – a true story and then I'm going to ask you to be a man and respect my confidences. I doubt that you have the strength to do it but we'll see."

She removed her glasses, as if to better see into the past. "I was the oldest of thirteen – six of us lived. My mother was in a wheelchair and my father was sick and couldn't work so I went into the shoeshop when I was fourteen."

"A shoe store? I thought you told me that you worked in some kind of factory when you were a kid."

"Not a shoe *store*, Paddy. In the shoe*shop* we didn't *sell* shoes, we *made* them – men's shoes and boots mostly. It was hard work, but there wasn't anyone else who could go out and make money. I worked all day, then came home and helped my sister, Betty, cook dinner for the family. On Friday, I gave my pay envelope to Mama — that was the only money we had." She glared at me or her mother or fate – I wasn't sure.

"My first job in the shop was sweeping the leather scraps into a bucket and carrying the bucket up three flights of stairs to the Fancy room – that's where they made decorations and such out of the scraps. From seven to seven every day except Saturday and Sunday – I got off at one on Saturday – I was bent over a damn little broom sweeping up scraps while the cutters worked on their tables over my head.

"When I was older, they moved me into the sewing rooms where I sewed uppers – that's where most of the girls worked 'cause it didn't take as much strength as building a shoe. I made more money there, because it was piece work. Do you know what that is?"

"I think so," I said, "you get paid for each piece you finish, right?"

"Yeah, I got two cents for each finished upper – and I worked fast, let me tell you. But when I got home, my hands hurt so bad I could barely make a fist. Still had to make dinner and clean up. 'Course dinner wasn't so hard to make when all we had to eat was potatoes." She sighed, "but we got by." Her voice, now softened, carried me back to those times…

"Miss Carter, you have a lovely, powerful voice, would you like to join the choir?" It was Reverend Mooney, the pastor of the church we went to. I liked his sermons a whole lot better than Reverend Chase the minister who was there before him. Reverend Mooney never screeched about sin and damnation but always preached about love.

"I'd be happy to, Reverend, but I don't have much time for practice and such. Mama's in a wheelchair and Daddy's sick…"

"Oh, I'm sure you can be spared for an hour or two on Wednesday night. Come at seven o'clock, won't you?"

Well, I wasn't so sure I could be spared but the idea of doing something besides working and sleeping had a powerful attraction. That Wednesday night, I rushed home from the shoeshop, washed up and changed into my second-best dress.

"Where you goin' Rae?" little Janey asked. "It ain't Sunday."

"I am going to sing in the church choir," I stated. "Reverend Mooney asked for me especially. Betty will feed you all."

"Aw, Betty always burns stuff. Why can't you do it?"

"Betty will learn, same as I did. And so will you in time, little girl."

More than a dozen men and women had already gathered in the church when I got there. I knew most of them from church so they were all very welcoming. They did confuse me a little when they asked about what parts I'd be singing. The sheet music they showed me might as well have been in Greek for all the sense it made to me.

Reverend Mooney welcomed me with his usual energy. "This is Mr. Schofield, our choir director," he said, turning to a small bald-headed man beside him. "Mr. Schofield, may I introduce Miss Rae Carter, a new talent for your group."

"Good evening, Miss Carter," the little man had a surprisingly deep voice. "Reverend Mooney tells me that you have a clear and well-modulated voice."

"Well," I stammered, "I like to sing and the Reverend…"

"Have you had any training?"

"Um, training? No."

"Very well, I'm guessing that you'd fit best with the altos." While he'd been talking to me, the other people had formed separate groups. Addressing one of them, he said "Altos, this is Miss Carter, she'll be joining you. Help her with her part, please."

The Queen

Paddy, that's how I began singing seriously. The family complained but I never missed a choir practice or a performance, not one.

It was at our spring concert that I met Eddie Meecham.

I know how much you like cars – you would have loved the one Eddie drove. He and his friends rolled into town in a huge, apple-green Marmon automobile. The auto created a sensation – the few cars in Drayton were mostly Model-T Fords and all black. It was the most beautiful machine most of us had ever seen. When the passengers stepped out in front of the Royal Hotel, they created a sensation that eclipsed their automobile The sharp double-breasted suits, spats and snap-brim hats were right out of the movies. And, best of all, they had money to spend.

This was the most exciting thing that had happened in town in years. Gossip – and there was a lot of it – had it that the group was part of a criminal gang – from Detroit or Chicago or Kansas City – on the run and hiding here in New Hampshire.

Drayton was a poor town full of poor people. Most everyone worked in the shoeshop or farmed. Families were big 'cause we needed all of them to support ourselves. If you got sick or hurt you only had your family to take care of you – warn't nobody else.

Can you imagine how impressed we were? When that big auto went by, everyone turned to see where it was going. The city boys pretty much took over the hotel – having a party every night with illegal liquor and as many people as they could get to come. And the people they wanted most were young girls. And most of the girls in town scrambled after them. Lots of mornings I'd go into the shop and see other girls so tired and sick from staying out drinking that they could barely work. I ask you, what did they think was going to happen when these men left? I wasn't no fool.

The choir's spring concert was a big deal in town. We'd set up in the park where church women would sell sweets and lemonade to bring in a little money for the church, you know. The children's choir had just finished when we heard a whole bunch of people talking and could see them looking at something – and wouldn't you know, it was the city boys, dressed to the nines, flowers in their lapels, smiling and tipping their hats to the ladies.

"Ladies, ladies!" Mr. Schofield cried, "it's time to go on. Hurry up! Hurry!" And we did. We marched out and got into the right places for Reverend Mooney to introduce us.

"Ladies and Gentlemen – and guests," he said with a nod to the newcomers, "it is my pleasure to introduce the First Congregational Choir led by Charles Schofield."

Since this was the first real concert I'd been in, I was nervous – and from where I was standing, I was looking straight at the flashy men from the big city. Would they laugh or make fun of us – they had certainly seen fancier shows than we could put on. Would I be able to sing at all?

"Look right over their heads," said Hildie Martin beside me, "I usually try to see in the second floor window of the mill." She gave me an encouraging smile and we began.

The Queen

When it was all over, a man came up to me – one of the city fellows. "You sing like an angel. Do you know jazz tunes as well?" He wasn't a very big man – shorter than I am with curly brown hair, sparkling blue eyes, a big smile, and a wonderful accent.

"I'm Eddie Meecham, from County Galway in Ireland, but late of Kansas City – my friends and I are staying in town for a little while." Then he stuck out his hand.

I let him take my hand – palm down like I'd been taught. "Thank you very much for the compliment but church choirs don't perform jazz numbers," I answered and walked away. I didn't want a reputation of being one of their girls.

"Perhaps, I'll see you around town," he called after me.

Now, Rae, I said to myself, there are too many people who depend on you to let those kind of feelings out – but he was cute in a mischievous way – I liked the way he talked, oh!

I did my best to forget about Mr. Eddie Meecham from Ireland, accent and all, but later, after the dishes were done and everyone else was in the parlor, my thoughts drifted back to him. He was very different from the young men I knew. He'd seen and done things, been places…

"Well, isn't it the songbird and her friends. 'Tis a fine evening, ladies, is it not?" He was waiting outside the shoeshop when I got off work. The other girls tittered and hid their faces behind their hands. "Might I escort you home, songbird?"

"No, Mr. Meecham, you may not!" I quickened my pace toward home.

"I'll just walk along here in the public thoroughfare, minding me own business – pay no attention to me 'tal."

And that's what he did. He strolled along beside us, but a few yards distant, showing not the slightest embarrassment. He continued even as, one-by-one, the girls turned off for their homes.

"I can't be calling you Songbird forever, Miss – surely you have a Christian name?"

"I do, but not for you, sir."

"Her name's Rae Carter!" laughed Dolly Singleton as she left the group. "And she lives a way up on the hill." Then she scampered off home.

"Rae Carter, is it? Ray like a ray of sunshine – which you surely are?"

"Just Rae and I'd thank you to leave me alone, Mr. Meecham."

"Very well, Miss Carter, if that's your wish, I have naught but to obey." He turned and strolled back toward the center of the village.

"He really likes you, Rae. Why are you being so cruel to him?" asked Cornelia Selfridge. Cornelia was my closest friend and worked in stitching same as me.

"I won't have anything to do with those fly-by-night city boys. I know what they want and I know they'll be gone in a few weeks or months. My people need me – you understand that, don't you?"

"Of course – but wouldn't it be fun to do *something* before we're old?"

I didn't answer. Getting out of this town and having a life of her own was the dream of every girl in town – but it would never come true. We would take care of our families until we married and added a husband and children to the ones who depended on us. The Eddie Meechams of the world offered only false hope then soon enough became a path to shame and ultimate abandonment.

My God he was persistent though – every evening, there he was. As the weather got warmer, he traded his snap-brim fedora for a Panama, the dark worsted suits for linen. He paced along with us, while I steadfastly ignored him – but it got harder and harder. Sometimes he serenaded us with sad Irish songs. Other times he entertained us with stories of his homeland or other places he had been. All the while he maintained a proper physical distance.

Cornelia changed it all. It was a fine late-June evening and Mr. Meecham had just finished a song about lost love when Cornelia began belting out *I Want To Be Happy* that we'd learned from the radio. She was in the choir as well and we'd clowned around with harmonizing to it. She poked me in the shoulder and forced me to pick up my part. Eddie responded with *Five Foot Two, Eyes of Blue* and then all of us, including Eddie, tried *Manhattan*.

"Oh, Mr. Meecham," said Cornelia, "you ought to hear Rae do *Always* – it'll bring tears to your eyes.

"Indeed." And he began the song, "I'll be loving you…"

So Eddie Meecham and I sang a duet on the side of the road, causing the dogs to howl, chickens to scatter and scandalizing the nearby farm families. I was done.

After that, it wasn't long before we went dancing together and drinking together. I met his friends and began spending most of my spare time at the Royal. A couple of professional dancers from Manchester who could sing a little bit taught me to dance a little bit and we began to put on shows for fun. Pretty soon people were coming in from other towns to hear us – and drink and spend money. That was my first taste of applause – I drank it up the way the customers were drinking up their booze.

Working in the shoeshop put food on the Carter table but it made doing shows that didn't even start until nine at night really hard, even for a woman as young as I was. Eddie wanted me to concentrate on being a singer so he said he'd take care of my family if I quit the shoeshop. We had a wonderful summer. Since the big Marmon belonged to one of the other men, Eddie bought a 1923 Franklin roadster so we could travel around by ourselves. We went everywhere in that little car – even up into Canada.

On these long-distance adventures we talked a lot and I found out what an exciting life he'd already had.

"Eddie, why did you leave Ireland? You make it sound like heaven," I asked. We'd stopped to picnic in the shade of an old maple tree. He'd loosened his collar and I'd taken off my hat while we ate and now were just relaxing in the mild breeze.

"Well, it is something like heaven but it's also something like hell. 'Tis a hard place, *Macushla*, especially the west counties, poor rocky soil, steep hills, and harsh weather." He looked across the pasture to where it was cut by a small creek. "Not so different from here, if you must know."

"*Macoosla*? What does that mean?"

"*Macushla*, girl, it means 'my beloved'"

My heart expanded with love for him but I just continued our conversation "But when you talk about how green it is…"

"Ah, yes, 'tis green enough and the land holds you to itself – even as you struggle to make your living. Difficult to explain – perhaps some day you'd like to visit?"

"You'd take me? That would be wonderful!"

He went on to explain that we'd have to wait awhile. He'd been an IRA soldier and fought in the Easter Rising in 1916 – and continued against the "damned Black and Tans" until he had to leave in 1919.

"That's where I became familiar with the Thompson gun," he told me, "'tis truly a fearsome weapon. A great gift from our friends in America and a great horror for the English patrols." His eyes became hard, "Then I was informed on. I barely escaped."

He landed in New York and found work as a laborer. Unsatisfied, he drifted west and ended up in Chicago in 1921 and later in Kansas City where some friends from the old country were making money subverting Prohibition.

"Such foolishness," he snorted, "denying a man drink – you might as well deny him air to breathe."

"Liquor wrecks families and dooms many to the lowest levels of society," I argued.

"Sure, if a man can't hold his liquor, but there's many things that are evil if over indulged…" He leaned over and kissed me. "For example…"

On the way home, he explained that it was robbing banks that bothered him, not the liquor business. Using his skill with a machine gun to protect a load of booze was, in his mind, nothing more than protecting property. To steal people's earnings was somehow different.

"You feel bad for the banks?" I asked. "They own everything – maybe they should share some of the wealth with us."

"And where does the money come from, *Acushla*, but from ordinary people?"

"No, it's money that the rich have screwed out of the poor. Robbing a bank is just taking some of it back."

"Jaysus! For a Yankee, you're quite a Bolshevik, aren't ya now?"

"I know what's right, is all."

It was robbing banks that forced them to "go on the lam" as he said. The Chicago mob had become more aggressive, forcing competitors to either join them or be driven out of the liquor business. If a gang resisted too strenuously, they were murdered. A war for control of illegal liquor raged all across the upper Midwest. Every morning big city papers carried stories about bodies being found in alleys and cellars – often with lurid photos.

"The gang and I were making good money, but there weren't but eight of us – how were we to fight Chicago?"

"Me and Sailor argued and argued about what to do – he was for getting out of the booze business and I wanted to work something out with the Eyetalians."

"Sailor?" I asked. "Was he in the navy?"

"Naw, we called him 'Sailor' after he damn near drown trying to ferry a load of booze across Lake Michigan from Canada. Had to be rescued by the American Coast Guard, he did. 'Course the booze was already on the bottom of the lake, so they brought him to shore and told him he should learn more about sailing before he tried the lake route again."

Sailor prevailed and their little gang of Irish criminals began a short-lived robbery spree. When they robbed the National Bank of Bloomington, Missouri, they were interrupted by two policemen. In the gunfight two of the gang members were shot along with three bank customers.

"That sent us scurrying as fast as ever we could to sanctuary in your lovely state," he said.

"But why New Hampshire?"

"Because, *Macushla*, the State of New Hampshire has a charming independent streak which includes not concerning itself with crimes that may have been committed outside its borders." He concluded, "So, here I am with you, me darlin'."

In the late fall, as the weather got colder, Eddie's friends got restless. Money was running low and small-town pleasures were wearing thin. Sailor and the rest of the gang wanted to head out, figuring that the law had forgotten about them by now. They could just change their names and relocate to more exciting places – maybe California.

Eddie wanted to stay with me. He'd saved most of his share of the gang's profits and had stashed it in a bank in Detroit – "just like a regular business man," he said.

Sailor and the others pressured him to help them get some traveling money by robbing a bank in nearby Manchester. Honor-bound, he joined them for this job – his last, he said. He left me and another girl at an old cabin, promising to come back soon.

Gram said, "They got away with the robbery, but the cops followed them to the cabin where we were waiting and raided the place. They just started shooting – never said they were the police or nothing. Cops are supposed to identify themselves and give you a chance to surrender – all they wanted to do was kill us."

####

"We, Gram? You were there?"

"Of course I was there." Her color came up a little, "I was going to have a baby and we were going to get married. We weren't going back to Drayton."

Eddie tried to surrender. I think it was because of me – he wanted to protect me and the baby. He went out of the cabin with his hands up and that Thompson gun in plain sight over his head.

The Queen

"He yelled, "Don't shoot! We're coming out. Don't shoot!" That cop just shot him down. Eddie fell there in the dooryard. He died right in front of me. If I'd been a better shot, that damn cop would have died, too. I emptied my revolver at him but didn't hit anything. J. Pete, another member of the gang, took the gun away from me and threw it in the stove so's they wouldn't know I'd shot at them.

The cops handcuffed and searched us, then shoved us into a paddy wagon – even J. Pete, who was bleeding all over the place. The last thing I saw before the doors closed was that cop standing over Eddie posing for a God damned picture! I really should have practiced with my pistol more.

When we got to jail, they searched us again – at least this time it was a lady cop – photographed and finger printed us, then put me and the other girl in a cell separate from the men. I found out later that J. Pete died there in the jail – bastards!

The cops took me out of the cell later and questioned me about Eddie and the bank robbery and the other girl. "How long had I been with them? Who were they? What other jobs had they pulled. Was I at the bank when they robbed it?" It went on for hours but I didn't say nothin'.

At trial a month or so later, I was convicted as an accessory to robbery after the fact and sentenced to eighteen months in prison. They let me out in six 'cause of the baby. I didn't have any place to go. My family was shamed but they finally took me back in. I hated it –people looking at me and talking about me behind my back. But I had a child – what was I going to do? After I had the baby,

I went back to the shoeshop and left little George – I named him after my poor sick father – with my mother.

#####

By the time my boy was two years old, I knew I needed to get him out of Drayton. If we stayed here, he'd grow up to be just like the stupid, shuffling nobodies that lived there. I was pretty sure I could safely go for Eddie's money after all this time. I could use it to get a start somewhere else and still take care of my mother and the rest of the family. With the little bit of money I had and the paper Eddie'd written out giving me the right to his money, I traveled to Detroit.

This was 1931, the bank Eddie had put all his money in had failed. His nest egg had disappeared. I didn't even have enough money for the train back home and had to go to one of Eddie's gangster friends for help. He didn't have much money either but he helped me get a job singing at a club and found me a place to live. I made enough to send money home for George and the family and did what I had to do for almost two years.

My signature was closing my act with *Always* – the song Eddie and I had sung all those years ago. A man came in one night and convinced me to make a recording of that song. It was never much of a seller but it got me enough attention to meet an agent who got me better jobs. In the end, he booked me into clubs in the Boston area – closer to George. I went home to see him as often as I could but it was almost harder seeing him then having to leave again. He looked like Eddie but wasn't Eddie.

#####

The Queen

My grandmother shook her head, got up and went to the stove and put the kettle on. "You want tea, Paddy?"

"Ah, yeah, that would be good." I didn't want her to stop the story but it was clearly opening old wounds. She didn't seem to be as angry with me as she had been at first – I decided to sit quietly and wait.

She fussed around with the teapot and cups. "Would you like some cookies? I'm going to have a couple."

"Sure, Gram, that would be great."

She brought the cups and teapot to the table. "Can you see why I didn't want anyone prying into this?"

"I guess…" I didn't really but was hoping to avoid any further disagreement with her – she still scared me. "So, did you meet Grampa Sprague in Boston?"

"Not really in Boston, but in a club not too far away…"

By 1936 everyone was poor – liquor was legal again, but no one seemed to care anymore. My club dates were harder to get and I was tired of it. I was singing more to drunk people than to people who were having fun and maybe had too much to drink. My audiences weren't happy – or maybe they just weren't happy with me, I don't know. As long as I was making money, I didn't care.

I do know that going on stage wasn't as exciting as it had been. I had a tiny little room in a woman's hotel in Cambridge. And I was sending most of what I made back to my mother. Most days I slept until two in the afternoon, then went to wherever I was booked to rehearse a little and eat something before the show. After crawling home at two or three in the morning, I'd flop in bed and do the whole thing over again the next day. If I didn't have a show that night, it was even worse – all I could do was sit around and hope I'd get another booking.

I was booked as a regular at Mancuso's, a big restaurant and night club in Boston doing two shows a night, four nights a week. For that I got thirty dollars and a free dinner on the nights I had a show. The money wasn't great, but it was enough to keep my family from starving.

I liked sitting in the main room before opening – the lights were dim, the brass bases of the lamps gleamed, glassware sparkled and the velvet chair cushions looked rich and elegant. Sitting alone in my personal cone of light, I finished my free steak and enjoyed the quiet and a cigarette. The room wouldn't open for an hour yet and the piano player had left after we finished rehearsing. I could hear the waiters moving softly around in the dark adjusting this or rearranging that. I was wondering if I could afford a drink, when this guy in uniform came up to the table.

"Hi...um...I, ah...I saw your show...and...Oh, Miss Carter, you were wonderful! So I...ah...I came back tonight." He was tall with nice eyes and cute in a bashful way.

"Why thank you, soldier, would you like to sit down for a minute? I don't have to go back to get ready for the show for another twenty minutes or so. Why don't you keep me company?" I caught the eye of the waiter and we ordered coffees.

"You sing so beautiful, I could listen to you for hours," the young man said.

"Soldier, I'm flattered, but I'm guessing you don't have a whole lot to judge by."

"Oh, Miss Carter, I'm not a soldier…"

"Well you're doing a fine imitation – what are you an usher or something?"

"No, Ma'am, I'm a marine."

He stated that fact so proudly. He seriously thought the difference between the Army and the Marine Corps was critical, even when we weren't at war any more. "Okay, Mr. Marine, what do you do with yourself nowadays, the war's been over for twenty years."

"I don't know about that – I spent three years in Nicaragua and I'm pretty sure those were real bullets whizzing by my head."

"Where's Nicaragua? And why were people shooting at you?"

"It's in Central America and we were there 'cause the President said to go. Thought I was goin' to China, too, but ended up on the Pennsylvania."

"In Pennsylvania?"

"No, on the Pennsylvania – the battleship. I'll be getting out pretty soon though – less than a year."

He was a nice guy and the first in a long time that wasn't trying to get something off me. For that reason I wished I could get to know him a little better but had to get ready for the show. "I've enjoyed talking with you – maybe you'll come back some time – but I need to get ready for the show now."

The conversation gave me a little lift while I changed into my stage gear – ridiculously expensive and terribly fragile but it's what people expect. Then the make-up and headband – what a production! I never got used to it. Seems like, if you could sing, you ought to be able to just sing and not have to get tricked out like a hoochie-coochie girl – gives men the wrong idea. Every night, usually after the second show, I had to slap some lug's face or stamp on his toe. I wouldn't wear it at all except that's what the bosses expected. Milt, the guy who owned this club, even told me to "shake it a little – give the guys something to think about." That's the last thing I wanted my audience to be thinking about. But what are you going to do – girl's got to make a living.

I was still sending most of my pay back to take care of George and my family. The last letter from my mother told me that no one in the family was working any more. My brother Arthur was considering heading out to California but his wife wouldn't let him go. My whole family and my son were living on odd jobs, what they could grow in the back yard, and the money I sent them. If I had to "shake-it" to keep this lousy gig, I would. I tried not to think about what would happen if I lost this job – I hadn't had an offer for a booking anywhere else in months. Guess I'd have to stop being so quick to slap faces.

My uniformed admirer was in the audience for my first show. I saw him after my first number, clapping and hooting – he was standing way in the back where the cover charge was lowest, but making enough noise to be heard way up here.

He showed up again the following Tuesday. There was no show that night so the big room wouldn't open for dinner until eight. The new piano player Milt hired and I were rehearsing and working out the breaks– the new guy wanted to jazz things up a little too much but, at least, he was sober. Even though the room was closed, don't I look around and find my marine standing right beside me?

"Miss Carter," he said, "could I take you to dinner?"

Since I wasn't working that night, I didn't get the free dinner that came with the job, in fact, I only had about a dollar twenty to get me through 'til the end of the month. A free dinner was worth spending some time with my marine, as I was beginning to think of him.

"Dinner, huh?" I sucked in my lips, "Dinner? I don't know…"

"I'll take you anywhere you want to go, Miss Carter…a long as it isn't *too* expensive…I only have my pay…"

"Where were you planning on taking me…what is your name anyway?"

"Ah, Jeffrey, Ma'am, Jeffrey Sprague. I thought we'd just eat here."

I touched his arm. "I'm sick of this place but I know a nice restaurant where we can get steaks and it won't cost you a million – it's just down the street."

I gave him my arm and guided him to Goodman's. We both had steaks and ate like longshoremen. He told me about Nicaragua and how he drifted into the marines. When he told stories about some of the characters he met, his laugh showed me a gorgeous smile – it took up his whole face. We both came from poor people so that neither of us got much of a start in life – his step-father kicked him out when he was fourteen. Finding the Marine Corps was, according to him, the best thing that ever happened. I talked about going into the shoeshop at fourteen but skipped over Eddie Meecham. We had fun – for an hour or so, I wasn't worrying about my life. I could feel a genuine affection for Jeffrey growing in my heart.

We met a few more times over the next weeks, continuing to enjoy each other company. As the time I spent with Jeffrey became more important to me, my livelihood became more precarious. Soon after Jeffrey and I started seeing each other, Milt cancelled the Thursday night shows and cut the band back to just a trio – it wouldn't be long before he decided that he couldn't afford me.

Fear of destitution was a constant companion – it's hard not to be afraid when grown men were competing with each other to split wood or deliver newspapers. The Works Progress Administration was created by President Roosevelt to try to get people back to work – even musicians and singers. The WPA had a program called the Federal Music Project, that hired musicians, singers and dancers to perform and teach and paid twenty-three dollars a week. I applied but, strangely, they never even checked to see if there were any positions available – they just turned me down. No one said anything but I figured that my trouble with the law was the problem. So I knew that Public Relief might reject me, too, if I applied.

What would my family do without the money I sent home? What would little George do? Losing my job would take away the only money that kept the family off the bread line. Milt wouldn't say so but it sure looked like my days of singing at the club might be ending soon.

While my marine's innocence and optimism was sometimes irritating, I depended more and more on him and his positive attitude.

Portsmouth Naval Prison, where he was stationed, was only about an hour's train ride from my little place in Cambridge.

"Duty at the prison is great," he claimed. "I get liberty almost every week and can come down from Portsmouth to see you."

"You ever get tired of guarding all those prisoners?" I asked him one night as much out of boredom as anything. "Seems like it would get you down – bad people all around you all the time."

"No, not at all. Most of them aren't all that bad – they broke the Navy's rules or stole some little thing from another sailor – easy things to accept." He paused for a moment, "I don't like the deserters, though – they joined up, then changed their mind and took off. They let everyone else down. They weren't faithful to the oath we took."

"You don't have really bad people like murders and such in your prison? I'm surprised."

"A few really bad ones, I guess, but not that many really – mostly the men are sorry for whatever it was they did and glad they're not out on the street right now."

"What do you mean?"

"They get three hot meals and a warm, dry place to sleep – better'n a lot of people nowadays."

While no one knows how awful it is to be locked up like an animal, I can understand that it might look better than sleeping in a field somewhere. The newspapers said things were getting better, but you couldn't prove it by anyone I knew. My bank account sure wasn't getting any fatter.

I knew he was going to ask me to marry him – or maybe I was afraid he was going to ask – afraid that I would have to say yes. I needed the security my marine offered but my feelings weren't the same as those I'd had for Eddie. I was still young enough to want to let my heart rule my head. This time, I had to do what I had to do.

"Just like always, there were people depending on me," she sighed.

When Eddie proposed, I leaped into his arms barely able to catch my breath long enough to say yes. With him, I was always on the verge of a shiver – my heart racing every time he touched me. When we were apart I actually ached for him and when he was killed I would have happily died with him.

Would I being doing the right thing, holding on to a man just because he was solid and treated me like a lady? Would he be happy with me after we were together awhile? What would happen if I ran into another man that made me feel like Eddie had?

I realized that I didn't have the luxury of worrying about those questions. I had a son and other people who depended on me – if he asked, I'd say yes. I'd make him a good wife. I had no choice. I had to do it. So I took all of the things I'd kept to remind me of Eddie and the life I used to live, wrapped them carefully, and put them, along with my memories, in this little chest and hid it.

When he finally did ask, it wasn't that hard to answer.

"Rae, you are the most beautiful and exciting woman I've ever met. I love you and I want to marry you." He lowered his head and said quietly, "Rae Carter, will you marry me?"

"Jeffrey, you know that I have a son…"

"Stop," he said. "Little George won't be a problem for me."

"Do you understand that you'll have a ready-made family? If you don't want one, I'll understand." I was sure he hadn't thought seriously about ending up with a wife and a seven-year old son.

"Well, I figured all along he'd come live with us…wouldn't that be all right? I'll be a good father to him, I promise."

My heart lurched, "Oh, Jeffrey, you're too good -- I would be thrilled to be your wife."

"You would? Really? I'm so happy," he yelped. He grabbed me and swung me around. "We'll have a great life together – can we do it soon? I don't want to wait!"

"Slow down, Jeffrey – where will we live? I don't want to give up my career – however pitiful it has become – and we have to think about George and where he'll go to school and such."

"We'll get married first – as soon as we can, if that's all right with you. Then I'll apply for a married housing on base or an allowance. We'll let George finish out the school year in Drayton, then start him in the new school next year. That way you can come back here for your shows…what's wrong?"

"…nothing…I hadn't thought…" Suddenly the thought of giving up my little apartment hit me like a punch in the stomach…I wouldn't have anything that was just mine.

"See, I have to be on duty at least five days a week and you only have two shows a week now…" He looked at me with sad, puppy-dog eyes as if I might take his bone away.

"Yes, of course – that makes sense…" Then I faced reality, "You're right it would be dumb to pay rent on two places. I don't know why I didn't see it right off."

"And while George is finishing school, we can get the apartment fixed up – base housing can be pretty beat up but I'm handy and a good painter. We'll have the place looking great by the time George comes to live with us." His excited description suddenly stopped, "You don't think he'll mind living with us, do you?"

"My marine, you are so silly sometimes – George will be so happy to finally have a father that the hard thing will be to keep him in Drayton long enough to finish the school year.

And so it was, we spent April and May painting and papering, scouting for second-hand furniture, borrowing some linens from my mother and aunts. I took the train down to Boston for shows or rehearsal. Coming home late on the train was tough and I didn't like it – I wondered how much it would really cost to get a little place of my own. Milt fixed that for me – he shut down the show entirely, fired the musicians, dancers and me.

Living on Jeffrey's pay wasn't easy, but it was steady. We could shop at the PX and Commissary and Jeffrey spent nothing on clothing and we got by. I came to look forward to him coming home to tell me about his day and we'd listen to our little radio. For the first time in my financial life, I felt safe.

####

The three of us had a wonderful summer – George loved living near the ocean – the base was on an island so he could see it whenever he wanted. We often took the trolley down to the beach and had a picnic and played in the water – it was pretty funny since I couldn't swim a stroke and neither could Jeffrey. The water was too cold for anything more than paddling for a few minutes anyway.

No one wanted summer to end – I had never been able to spend so much time with my boy – but, in September, George went off to his new school without complaining. After a week or two he confessed that he didn't like it any more than his old school but there wasn't anything to be done about it.

One afternoon between Thanksgiving and Christmas I was knitting and listening to *Days of Our Lives* on the radio when I heard someone knocking on our door. It was beastly hot in the house – the Navy heated all of the houses with steam from the plant and you never could tell if you were going to freeze or roast so I had the door propped open to get a little cold air in.

"Yoo hoo," a woman's voice drifted in, "Hello, anybody home?"

A young woman was standing at the door with a baby on her hip and a plate in her hand.

"Come in, come in," I opened the door all the way. "Let me just turn off the radio."

"No need, I'm normally listening to it, too," she said. "Amanda and I just wanted to come over and introduce ourselves. These are for you, your husband, and your little boy," and she handed me a plate of cookies. "We don't want to interrupt you, but I saw the inside door open – like we all do – and thought it would be okay to just knock."

Her name was Marion and we became fast friends after that, spending many afternoons together. Sometimes, I'd watch Amanda so that Marion could go shopping or she'd keep an eye on George. Sometimes we'd get together with a couple of the other wives and play cards in between taking care of children. They were mostly younger than me, but it was wonderful to finally have friends around.

Marion and her husband had a Victrola and some records and the two of us would play records and sing sometimes while the men were at work. I'd tell her about singing on stage and some of the funny things that happened – like the time I caught the heel of my shoe in the hem of my slinky dress as I walked on stage. I had definitely, I told her, given the boys more of a show than I planned on.

"I can't imagine being in front of all those people – with or without the top of my dress," Marion giggled. "I would just freeze – then die of shame."

"But, if you can get them to clap, it's wonderful!"

"Do you miss it much?"

"I miss singing on stage, but I don't miss worrying about my job, or being pawed by men, or being alone all the time. This is better – and I've got my little boy with me. I'm just an ordinary housewife now."

Jeffrey's hitch was up in August of 1938 and his commanding officer really wanted him to re-up – said he needed experienced marines for what was coming. We both agreed that "what was coming" was a good reason for him to muster out. After all, Jeffrey had served for twelve years. After fighting in different places all around the world, he didn't want to do it again.

"You don't think I'm being a coward, do you, Rae?"

"No, Jeffrey, I don't – you've already done your part, it's time someone else stepped up to 'whatever's coming'."

After Jeffrey mustered out, he got a good job with an automobile dealer that sold Hudsons and Terraplanes. Times were getting better and people had money to buy cars again. We rented a little house in town close to the main gate – I didn't want lose my friends from the base – and settled in. It wasn't until later that I realized that my life had become ordinary – I even had friends and time to enjoy them.

Jeffrey did well at the dealership and gave me a great present. He brought home a 1932 Plymouth sedan. We had a car again, hard-used, upright and not in the least streamlined but a car! The driver's seat beckoned – a Plymouth wasn't as impressive as a Marmon or even my old Franklin – but oh, the freedom!

That old car was my magic carpet. Some days, if the housework was all caught up, I'd drop Jeffrey off at work and George at school and just drive and drive. Behind the wheel with gas in the tank, I could go anywhere! San Francisco, New Orleans, New York City – all I had to do was put my car in gear and head out – my only limitations were time and fuel.

No longer bound to a stove or a mop – or a husband or a son – I was free. No one could make me go (or stay) anywhere. I could choose. Choose to drive to California or head back to a loving family – my choice, no one else's. That old Plymouth and I covered some ground. In the end, I always decided to go home – because I wanted to.

Happiness agreed with me – I threw myself into the mundane chores of housework – why not? It was my house. There was enough time to take a little money from my friends playing canasta or gin and there was always Jeffrey and George. I noticed that I was even getting fat – too much of a good thing, I guess.

George was one of the few things that Jeffrey and I argued over. He thought George was spoiled and needed to toe the line more closely and I was just so happy to have him with me after all the time apart, I couldn't discipline him.

"Jeffrey, he's a little boy – you can't expect him to be a little marine! Think about your father – do you want to drive George out when he's fourteen? Is that what you want?" I demanded.

"Rae, I'm not being unreasonable – the boy sasses you and is disobedient and there's no reason for you to put up with it."

"Well, Jeffrey, he's my son and I'll raise him as I see fit. If that doesn't suit you, you can leave. I've made my way before and I can do it again."

He insisted, "Rae, you're spoiling him. You'll turn him into a little mama's boy. All I'm saying is that you should say 'no' once in a while."

"And you're picking on him. I told you from the start that I had a son and he was coming with me. That's that!"

And that was that. The only time Jeffrey ever disciplined George was when George called me a "mean old bitch." Jeffrey paddled George's bottom so bad that the boy had to stand up to eat his meals for days. Other than that, George and Jeffrey stayed out of each other's way for the next three years.

Then my happy little normal life changed again. Jeffrey had gotten malaria while he was serving in Nicaragua. We all thought he'd gotten over it. Then one morning he was so weak he couldn't get out of bed. The doctor told us that there was really nothing he could do and that, as Jeffrey got older, he would have these flare ups. According to the doctor, they were nothing to worry about.

That was easy for him to say "...nothing to worry about..." but what were we supposed to do while Jeffrey couldn't work? He did try – I'd drive him to the dealership in the morning but, by lunchtime, I had to go get him and put him to bed. I didn't know what to do. I checked in the tobacco tin we used to hold grocery money – all we had was six dollars and thirty-two cents.

I was right back where I started after Eddie was killed – except now I had both Jeffrey and George to take care of. Nobody was going to help me as always, I did whatever I had to do.

I knitted up the yarn I had on hand into baby booties and went around the neighborhood to see if I could sell them. That day I made four dollars! That four dollars got me some more yarn, some knitting needles and crochet hooks, a few buttons and thread. I sold that stuff and made some more booties and bought some more stuff until I had a little store going. We moved to a place closer to the center of town where I could have the store on the first floor and live in the apartment on the second and third floors. It warn't much, but we were warm, dry and had food on the table.

By then, Paddy, your father was running loose. He never liked school much and I didn't have time to chase him down. My father came to live with us after my mother died and he was supposed to take care of George while I was running the store. Of course, Grandad was probably a bigger kid than your father – he shot a neighbor lady in the rear end with a BB gun, then quickly handed the gun to George so he'd take the blame. But what could I do?

I can tell you what I'm not going to do, now, Paddy my boy. I'm not going to make the mistakes with you that I did with your father. You *will* have to take the consequences of your misbehavior and in the future you *will* obey my wishes and you *will* stay out of trouble. Is that clear?

I nodded, still half under the glamour of old times.

She closed the chest. "I think you probably know that during the war, I got work on the shipyard. I ran a turret lathe. Made good money, too."

"Gram, I don't know what a turret lathe is," I admitted.

"It's a big machine that cuts parts out of big pieces of steel. I was good at it, too. I made shafts for ship engines – on the sly, I also made those candlesticks on the table." She laughed, "they never found out about it either!"

I looked at the foot-high gleaming candle sticks. "You made these? Wow!"

"We had to, the men were all fighting." She hesitated for a moment, "Even George, joined up in the last year of the war. It was over before he had to go overseas, thank God."

She heaved herself up from the table. "Now put this chest back up in the attic and never open it again. Do you understand?" I nodded. "And remember, you don't always get to choose – all you can do is face what you have to do."

"I still don't understand, Gram – why haven't you ever talked about this?"

"Because I was ashamed, Paddy. I didn't expect anyone to understand that I had to do what I did. I had to take care of my family – there wasn't anybody else. I did what I had to do – just as I always have."

There were tears on her cheeks but she lifted her chin and repeated, "I did what I had to do."

"Why did you decide to tell me this – you could have just punished me?"

"Oh, I'm going to punish you, sonny, don't you worry about that. You just kept nosing around and you'll remember what that gets you."

"No, really, why tell me the whole story?"

"Because you have a choice to be as good and faithful a man as your step-grandfather – and you should know that life isn't always simple. If you live by his Marine Corps motto, *Semper Fidelis* – Always Faithful, you might grow up to be a good man.

Loving You Always

I welcomed the silence after crunching and rumbling over the gravel camp road for half an hour. As the tan dust settled over my car, the high-pitched *cheeezzzz* of cicadas welcomed us to camp. I leaned forward to peel my damp shirt from the car seat. We sat enjoying the quiet moment, the smell of hot sand and pine trees, and joy of each other's company. I drank in the heat. I think my service in Nicaragua and the Philippines must have permanently thinned my blood or maybe memories of those freezing days of my youth on the road so long ago made me hate cold weather.

Even in the summer, I could still feel the bite of the January wind through a tattered wool shirt and shiver. Rae touched my arm.

"Are you okay, Jeffrey?"

"Always."

The camp was set into the side of the steep hill running down to the lake. From the parking area, we looked down at the back of the camp and George standing in the doorway looking up at us. He already had a beer in his hand – at eleven o'clock in the morning! The grandkids wiggled past him to surge up the stairs toward us.

"Hi, Gram. Hi, Gramp," they chorused, "Do you want to go swimming?"

Rae smiled. "Well, kids, I might paddle my feet a little. Is it really that hot inside?"

"Yeah, Gram, it's pretty hot in the camp," Alice answered. "But it's nice in the water! We've already been in this morning."

"And we went fishing," Mary chimed in, "just off the dock though 'cause there's no gas for the boat."

The girls' older brother, Patrick, strolled up to the car to lean against the front fender. Cloaking himself in the jaded sophistication appropriate to a sixteen-year-old boy, he indulgently observed the antics of his sisters.

"Paddy," I said, "can you and the girls get the stuff out of the car while I help your grandmother down the stairs?"

"Sure, Gramp. Alice, Mary, give me a hand here."

Rae was surveying the wobbly, cement-block stairs down to the camp, hesitant to begin. It's always a surprise to me when I'm reminded of our ages – I expect her to Charleston at the drop of a hat or a drop of drink. Taking her arm, I guided her down the steps gently teasing her about getting old.

George finally put his beer down and rushed over to the foot of the stairs to help his mother.

"George, when in the hell are you going to fix these steps?" she snapped. "They've been like this for years. Someone's going to break their neck on them!"

"Oh, Ma, don't start."

"I'm not kidding, someone'll get hurt and then where will you be?"

"Okay, Ma. Come on in and have a cold drink." He looked up the stairs at his kids carrying boxes and grocery bags behind us. "Now what did you do? I told you that you didn't have to always bring food."

Reaching level ground, Rae stood up to her full five-feet-ten, "I never go anywhere empty-handed."

George gave me a "what are you going to do" look over her shoulder. "How are you, Dad? You feeling better?"

"Fine, George, just fine. There's some fruit in those bags that probably should be washed and put away." There wasn't any reason to get into a discussion of my health right now. They'd gotten the damned malaria under control and I felt pretty good, just tired sometimes.

Our daughter-in-law, Carol escorted us to comfortable chairs on the screen porch. "It'll be cooler out here, Gram," she said. "Can I get you a cold drink? Lemonade or a soda?"

When she came back with the sodas, she and George joined us to chat and catch up while the kids swirled around the camp and the docks down the hill from us. I was admiring the way Alice slipped through the water as she swam out to the float with Mary thrashing along behind her.

The afternoon sun glittered off the water and the girls' wet skin while they splashed and cannon-balled each other. On the hill below me I noticed my boat, looking like it had been abandoned to the elements. Upside down almost hidden in the puckerbrush, it obviously hadn't been touched since I had gotten sick two years ago. Like me, it was slowly rotting away.

As usual, I couldn't rely on George or his family for a god-dammed thing! He made a big deal of giving me the boat as a sixty-fifth birthday present, then just heaved it into the brush and forgot about it while he sat around drinking beer.

I didn't want to spoil Rae's visit with her grandchildren, but her son's irresponsibility infuriated me. Nothing ever changes, I guess. He was a spoiled little boy when I first met him at seven years old and hadn't grown up yet. Well, I wasn't so decrepit that I needed to rely on him to maintain my boat.

Paddy was leaning against the doorframe between the kitchen and the screen porch, imitating his father's favorite pose. "Paddy," I said. "Do me a favor, clear some of that puckerbrush from around my boat, will you?"

"Well...sure, Gramp. Right now?"

"Yes, I'd like it done when I get back from the hardware store."

George looked at me, surprised, "You just got here, Dad, so what do you need at the store?"

"I've got to get some things." Turning to Paddy, "You *will* get that cleared out like I asked?" He nodded.

####

When I got back to camp with scrapers, sandpaper, paint and such, Paddy had already cleared three feet of space all the way around the boat leaving plenty of room to work.

George came down shortly after I started scraping the flaking paint off my boat. "Dad, you don't have to do that," he said.

"Someone has to, George – just like I've been telling you for years. Do you remember when you left your new bicycle out in the rain when you were a kid?"

"Geez, Dad, do we have to go over this again?"

"What did I tell you?"

In exactly the same tone he used when he was eleven, he recited, "Little jobs are important. If I don't take care of my things, pretty soon I won't have anything."

"And, do you remember what you said?"

"You're not my father and you can't make me do anything," he ground out.

"What happened then?"

"You spanked me and Mama yelled at you – told you never to do it again."

"George, since that time, I've never forced you to do anything – I'm not starting now." I took out my anger by scraping even more furiously. "My boat is going to be scraped and painted today and that's the end of it."

Turning his back on me, he stomped off up the hill. I could hear Rae giving him hell but it didn't matter to me anymore. My anger had gotten the better of me and I was ashamed of myself, which made me even angrier. Sending paint chips flying, exposing clean bare wood helped me calm down at little but I was still furious when Paddy shuffled down the hill and stood shifting from one foot to the other.

"Can I help you, Gramp? I'm sorry," he mumbled, looking at his sneakers.

"For what, Paddy?"

"I feel like I should have done something before now."

"Yeah, Paddy, I *do* think you should be a little sorry." Taking a deep breath, I said, "but I can sure use the help. Grab one of those scrapers and start on the other side, would you?"

It was hard to be stay mad at the boy – he didn't know any better. George had never taught him to think of anyone else. We scraped in companionable silence for a while, Paddy on one side of the boat and me on the other. Working together and the pleasure of a task with clear results loosened my tongue.

"Let me tell you, Paddy, when I was on my own, before I went in the marines, I worked for a logger named Jake Slater. After working all day in the freezing cold, he insisted that we clean and sharpen the saws every night.

We'd sit in front of the woodstove and chat about the day or just smoke in silence while working on the saws.

I was about your age and couldn't see why we spent so much time doing it – after all, they didn't get that dull in one day. I didn't exactly complain, but there were other things I'd rather have been doing. The next day, Jake gave me an old rusty saw to use. I've never worked so hard in my life! The damn thing wouldn't cut, then it would get stuck about every fourth stroke. At the end of the day, I appreciated a nice clean sharp saw."

We scraped in rhythm for a moment.

"Couldn't you have just sharpened them when they needed it?" Paddy asked.

"That's the perfect question. Sure, the saws didn't get too dull in a day or even two or three but it's human nature to keep putting things off until you have a saw like the one Jake made me use. Then it takes hours to get it clean and sharp again. The easiest way to do anything, Paddy, is to make it part of your routine. It seems to me, that taking care of little things while they're still little makes everything go along smoothly."

Paddy and I worked hard for the next couple of hours, removing all the loose paint and sanding the hull smooth. After that, my back needed a rest. "What do you say, Paddy, ready for a break?"

"Sure am, Gramp. I'm going to get a cold drink. Can I get you something, too?"

"Yeah, and bring my pipe and tobacco, too, please."

We sat in the shade a little farther up the hill, smoking and enjoying the breeze. The boat still needed to be painted but we'd finished the bull work. My back told me that we should put it off for another time but that would leave the boat with bare wood exposed to the elements, really in worse shape than it had been. I certainly couldn't rely on anyone else to paint it. I also wanted Paddy to learn that a job three-quarters done is still not done.

"What do you think, Gramp, just need to paint it now, huh?"

"Yup, then we'll have to wait for the paint to dry before we turn it over to see what needs to be done on the inside." We wouldn't get any further than painting today but I'd feel better knowing that it wasn't sitting here rotting away. "Do you know if your father has any sawhorses around? I'd like to get the boat up off the ground."

Paddy discovered some beat-up sawhorses in the crawlspace under the camp that we struggled to get the boat on – I'd forgotten how heavy it was. While we were wrestling with the boat, I stumbled over a pile of tools concealed by the undergrowth and almost dropped it on my foot. Paddy was able to steady it while I regained my grip and we got it up and secured. I picked up the tools – several wrenches, a screwdriver, and a hammer – handed them to Paddy and told him to take them and put them where they belong. They were covered with rust from being left outside but could still be cleaned up and used.

Paddy returned with George's reply, "Dad said to just throw them away, Gramp. He's already bought new ones."

"Must be nice to have so much money you can just drop tools wherever you're at and buy new ones when you need them, huh?"

While we were painting, Rae and George's angry voices drifted down to us. Paddy kept glancing up at the windows then back at me. I ignored the argument and Paddy's desire for a comment. The two of them fighting like cats and dogs was nothing new.

"Why do they do that, Gramp?"

"Do what, Paddy?"

"Argue all the time. Don't they like each other?"

"Oh, they love each other – it's just that they are holding grudges that they can't let go of.

"What grudges?"

"Your father resents Rae for not being there for him when he was little and she feels cheated because she spent so many years supporting her family. Don't worry about it. Tell me about what you're planning to do when you get out of school."

"I don't really know. Probably join the marines like you and Dad." He wanted a reaction from me, I think.

"Your father and I had different experiences in the marines. What does he think about you enlisting?"

"He said, and I quote, 'You can go shoot gooks anytime. Go to school'." Paddy hesitated, "But he doesn't understand that I can't just decide to go to college – it costs a lot of money. He acts like it's all my responsibility so I'm going to disappoint him again."

123

This was delicate ground. If George didn't want him to enlist, I didn't want to contradict or criticize him. "Like I said, Paddy, we feel different about our service. As a marine, for the first time in my life, I was sure to get three meals a day and a warm place to sleep. I got better at reading and writing, got good medical care, hell, I even went to the dentist for the first time in my life. I saw some places and made some friends that I never would have. Your father had a rougher time."

"What do you mean, you were both in the war, right?"

"We were both in wars, but neither of us was in the one you're thinking of. I was in from '26 to '38 before World War II, and your father was in from '46 to '51, after World War II."

"But, Gramp, you both have combat medals – I've seen them."

"I fought in what they call the Banana Wars, Paddy, small unit stuff in the jungles and mountains in South America and the islands. Oh, the bullets were real enough and the fighting was hard, but nothing like your father's battles at Chosin Reservoir and the long retreat back to Pusan in Korea. I can understand why he wouldn't want you to get involved over in Viet Nam."

"Chosin Reservoir? What happened there?"

"Ask your father or look it up for yourself." There wasn't any point in trying to get a sixteen-year-old to understand the horror of a four-week, hundred-mile retreat in below-freezing temperatures under constant enemy fire – being afraid to leave the line of march even to answer the call of nature for fear of being caught by the Red Chinese. Let George tell him about that. Plus I'd done enough preaching for one day.

"We need to finish painting this boat, then I want to get something to eat and take a nap."

####

Paddy did enlist, fought overseas, and most of him came home. I say most of him because he left something of himself over there. The GI Bill got him through college. He married, had a child, divorced, took to booze then broke the habit – I'm not sure any of it made him particularly happy or unhappy.

The last time I saw him was in Florida after Rae and I moved down there. He had some business thing in Orlando and visited us while he was close by. When he came through the door of our trailer, the hardness in his eyes and the lines on his face shocked me. If anything, he looked more willing to kill than when he'd come home from Viet Nam ten years ago.

"Jesus, Paddy, you look like you've been rode hard and put away wet. What's up?"

"I don't know. Same old thing I guess."

"From the look on your face, maybe you ought to do something other than the same old thing."

"Always right to the heart of things, huh, Gramp?" He laughed, showing a little of the old Paddy. "It's nothing so bad. I'm making good money and doing a good job. What more can you expect?"

"Well, happiness, of course."

"I don't know, Gramp, that may be a tall order for me. How do you do it?"

"It's easy. I've been given the great privilege of taking care of the woman I love for nearly fifty years. I was in love with her from the moment I first saw her in the spot light of a crappy nightclub in Boston to this very minute."

"Geez, Gramp, that sounds like happily ever after and we know that isn't true."

"Of course it is! Whatever hard times Rae and I had were just more chances to show how much we loved each other. We took care of each other. I took her out of that dive in Boston and provided a home for her and George – she took care of me through half a dozen operations and a lifelong case of malaria. And, through it all, we had a great time."

Paddy indulged me with a smile but I could see that he didn't have the faintest idea what I meant. Rae entered the room and the conversation veered off into grandchildren and great grandchildren.

A few weeks after his visit, I headed out on my morning walk, not forgetting to pat Rae's inviting fanny and embarrassing her a little. I loved the early morning when the world is waking up and everything is yet to come.

Suddenly there was so much pain in my chest that I couldn't breathe. It was like someone was crushing me in a giant vice. Not so different from when I got shot in Nicaragua. Can't be a bullet, we're in an old folks trailer park, for god's sakes. Just in case, I struggled up against the door to block another shot if one came. The world fluttered before my eyes and the pain was absorbed by Rae, safe in our trailer, putting her heart into singing *Always* just to me. "I'll be loving you, always…"

Always.

Reality

Semper Fi

The whooshing sound from her severed windpipe was barely audible over the drumming of the rain. Hot arterial blood splashed over my hand while death spasms racked her body. The sudden stench of her bowels letting go signaled she was gone. – I let her fall.

My young Viet Cong guard had surrendered to her desire to watch her team leader torture an American marine. The leader, the woman my squad had dubbed the She-Demon, had left a trail of atrocities for us to follow and lead us into an ambush.

Seeking titillation in the pain of a helpless marine was my guard's second mistake. The first was doing a sloppy search that missed my grandfather's little folding knife. He gave it to me before he passed away when it was clear that I was going overseas – he told me to carry it for good luck.

"I carried it all the time I was in the corps," he said, "always brought me luck – and you can always use it to open C-rations."

It didn't bring me enough luck to stay out of the ambush that Charlie had set for our squad. Their positions had additional cover from the pouring rain and we were within thirty meters of them when the VC opened up.

The squad had to pull back leaving me, Carlson, and a couple of dead guys behind. The two of us were both in rough shape – he'd taken a round through the thigh and I had a punji stick jammed the length of my forearm with an eight-inch stump sticking out. The commie bastards had mined the ditches near the kill zone with these sharpened and barbed bamboo stakes – I'd dived right onto one.

The VC dragged us off and stripped us of everything but our pants and marine corps skivvies. Hands bound, barefoot and shirtless, we were marched down the trail by a rope around our necks.

Carlson, moaning from the pain, had to lean on me to walk at all. The VC drove us forward with slaps, kicks, and rifle butts but, before we'd traveled more than a couple of kilometers, he collapsed.

The She-Demon, an unimpressive-looking woman of indeterminate age, walked over to him and casually kicked him squarely on his wound – His scream was beyond anything I believed a human voice could make. She snapped orders in sharp Vietnamese. Her men hauled Carlson off in one direction while the young girl who had searched me when I was captured now grabbed the stub of bamboo sticking out of my arm. Using it as a leash, she dragged me into a clearing just off the edge of the trail and roped me to a tree.

As soon as my teenage guard was distracted by the lure of torture, I used my grandfather's knife to free myself and silence her. Mindlessly panicked, I scrambled into tall swamp grass that surrounded the clearing.

There was nothing I could do for Carlson except die alongside him. The rain rattling on the tall razor-edged swamp grass was loud but not loud enough to cover his pleas. "…no…no…please…" then a long piercing scream…

As I crawled away, the sharp grass scored my bare skin – a feast for clouds of stinging insects. I fell into a low ditch whose foul-smelling black mud I smeared on my face and body to camouflage my bright white skin and to protect me from the bugs. I hadn't gotten much further when the She-Demon yell from the clearing in accented English, "you will be caught and die slowly, Yankee Murderer."

Gunfire raked the grass around me spraying clippings and dirt while I lay belly flat in the ditch. I heard her order her soldiers deeper into the grass. The pounding rain covered any sound I made sliding alligator-like down the ditch on my belly but also covered the sounds of the searchers.

The stem of the damn punji stick slowed me down. I couldn't pull it out against the barbs and I couldn't cut the stem off one-handed. I could only try to protect it as I moved. I didn't see the vine drifting on the water's surface before it slipped between my arm and the stick. When it snagged, a bolt of red agony shot up my arm and through my heart. I must have fainted.

Coughing and choking I came back to consciousness face-down in the ditch water. Nice obituary, Paddy. He escaped from a Viet Cong torturer only to drown in three inches of filthy water.

The ditch ended in a swamp that forced me to struggle through a foot-deep soup of mud as well as the thick sharp-edged grass. Despite sauna of jungle heat, I was chilled to the bone and shivering in the pounding rain. To disguise my trail from the pursuing VC, I had to reach back every few meters to straighten the grass behind me.

I had to keep moving! Begging and screaming like Carlson was not the way I wanted to die. Eventually the mud and slop under me became firmer, promising dry ground somewhere ahead. My progress was pathetically slow – leaden arms and legs, labored breathing, and a throbbing wound. I wanted to just lie here until I died. Thoughts of the She-Demon behind me spurred me on toward higher ground.

Crawling with my eyes closed to keep the bugs out, I tumbled into a low spot only to find it already occupied by the body of a fallen American soldier. Mentally apologizing to him for the disrespect, I crawled toward the body to see if there was anything still on it that would help me. Dragged by a rope around my neck, marching barefoot over rough jungle trails had torn up my feet, maybe his boots…

A hand grabbed my ankle.

My heart jumped into my throat as I spun to face the new threat. The soaked and mud-covered marine holding my ankle shook his head and waved me away from the body. To hell with that! I needed those frigging boots.

When I turned back to get them, he hauled me bodily backwards.

"What the hell, man," I hissed.

My weak resistance couldn't stop him from pulling my good arm across his shoulders to help me stagger through the rain to a little tree-covered ridge. We huddled under the trunk of a fallen tree hidden from sight by the thick underbrush. Shivering and exhausted, I fell into a half sleep populated by VC and a grinning She-Demon with a bloody knife.

Night must have come and gone while I thrashed and moaned in my burrow. It didn't matter to me – I was riding fever dreams in and out of consciousness. In the daylight, my arm was bright red with pus oozing out from around the punji stick. The marine tried to cut away the protruding end of the stick but gave up when I couldn't hold back my screams. The best he could do was share a chocolate bar and help me drink some water.

Alternately sweating and shivering, I slept through most of that day. He stayed with me giving me small sips of water when I was awake enough to drink without choking. By the time darkness fell, I had become resigned to dying under that rotting tree.

"Leave me, man," I croaked, "it's over."

He didn't say anything just shifted his rifle and stared out into the darkness.

My dreams that night were of home – my family, the smell of pine and spruce, snow, the astringent bite of the frigid Atlantic – anything but the fetid reek of Vietnam.

Visions of both my father and grandfather in their marine uniforms floated through my head encouraging me not to give up, to remember that I was a marine. I just wanted it to be over.

Voices speaking Vietnamese woke me. The marine signaled me to be quiet while he peered through the rain. Oh shit, they've found us! My debilitated condition put escape out of reach for me, but there was hope for him. I touched his shoulder and nodded toward the ridge behind us. He pressed his hand over mine, shook his head, then calmly scooted forward into a firing position.

The approaching soldiers were close enough that I could hear them clearly through the rattle of the rain.

Pow! The marine's rifle spoke. He worked the action and fired again…and again…calmly selecting his targets not wasting any ammunition. I saw the muzzle flashes of dozens of rifles flickering through the rain as the enemy returned his fire. Damn! This couldn't be the She-Demon's twenty-man patrol – it was a company-size formation that had stumbled onto us. There could be as many as two hundred Viet Cong out there. Damn! Damn! Damn!

Suddenly the marine and I heard a new source of gunfire – the unmistakable rattle of American M-16's and roar of an M-60 machine gun. I lifted my five-hundred-pound head up enough to see American troops sweeping into the VC flank and driving them back through the swamp.

The strain of holding my head up was too much – I passed out again.

I came fully awake in a hospital bed with only dim recollections of being medevaced, then nothing until now. A uniformed woman with a stethoscope around her neck came to the side of my bed.

"You're awake – good. I'll get Lieutenant Moore," she said, "so be polite – he's the one who took that nasty hunk of wood out of your arm."

Lieutenant Moore was a tall black doctor who looked like he'd seen everything and hadn't liked any of it. After looking at my chart for a moment, he grunted before starting to remove the bandages from my arm.

"Let's see how this is coming along," he said half to himself. Then to me, "It looks like we're beating the infection. I didn't want to open your whole arm up for debridement and risk muscle and nerve damage so I pushed the damn thing all the way through. I thought the chance of a worse infection was worth taking and it looks like it worked out – have to keep a close eye on it for a few more days."

"Doctor, where am I?"

"Chu Lai. You came in yesterday and I'm the one who took care of you – got rid of the stick and dosed you up with antibiotics." He stopped removing bandages and smiled. "Don't bother to ask – we didn't keep the filthy damn stick as a souvenir."

"So I'm going to be okay?"

"Looks like it – 'course you're gonna have two nice scars to show your grandchildren."

He finished removing the dressing on my arm – the second wound was just below my elbow. "mm…mm..mm, yup, you're gonna have scars. Probably need to get a tattoo like Morelli's to hide this one," pointing to the still-oozing entrance wound.

"Show him your tat, Morelli," he said to the guy in the next bed who obligingly raised his arm to display the corps emblem in full color. The doctor laughed, "But not until this thing has healed." He started to leave, then turned back, "and we found these in your pocket."

He put my grandfather's knife on the side table and along with a rifle shell. "You a hunter?"

"No, why?"

"That's a thirty-aught-six shell – military hasn't used those since the 'Fifties. Figured it must be a good luck charm or something."

When I picked up the brass, I could tell that immediately that he was right, the case was longer and slimmer than the .30 caliber round we used now. Where the hell could it have come from? I must have picked it up in the field from ..."Yo, Doc, what about the other marine?"

"What other marine? You were all alone in some kind of a hole under a tree when they found you."

"Are you sure?" What had happened to the marine who dragged me out of that swamp?

Morelli spoke up, "the only thing we found, besides you and beaucoup gooks, was the body of a guy from the 173rd Airborne." He paused. "Of course the sonsofbitches booby trapped the body. Cost one guy a leg and put couple of hunks of metal in me. We didn't find no other marines."

I questioned everyone in the hospital including the corpsman who got me to the helo. No one saw another marine. Damn it, someone dragged me out of that swamp. When I find him, I'll have to show him the scars on my arm or the tattoo I get to hide…

My head spun. The marine who saved me had a marine emblem tattoo – one I was very familiar with, the one faded and shrunken on my grandfather's arm.

Then the scene under the log replayed in my mind. When the Viet Cong closed in on us, the marine had *worked the action* of his rifle between shots – something unnecessary with modern military rifles. The last bolt action rifle issued to US troops, the Springfield A3-O3, was replaced in the mid-'Thirties – and was chambered for the powerful thirty-aught-six cartridge – like the one in my hand.

Semper Fi, Gramp.

One More War

The house was ordinary enough, a little bungalow in a vast tract of little bungalows. I checked the number against my notes for the second time, got out of the rented Chevy, and walked as slowly as I could up to the front door.

I was here to lie to Dominick "Dom" Dombrowski's parents. I was going to tell them that he died instantly, that he never knew what hit him, that he was a good marine. I would not tell them the truth. He'd been a fuck-up and died screaming while he bled to death from a wound delivered by a Viet Cong 12.7mm machine gun. My attempt at medical treatment, putting a pressure bandage on his shattered leg, probably didn't do anything but prolong his agony. But, I was there when he died, he was a marine, and I owed the family.

The door was opened by a small worn woman in slacks and a man's flannel shirt. Everything about her was slightly faded – her blond hair thin and going grey, pale skin, thin bloodless lips with which she attempted a smile. "Yes?"

"Are you Dominick's mom? I was with him when he died and thought you might have questions."

Her face changed. As if the bones of her skull had shifted, her face became the visage of an avenging bird of prey. She pinned me with predator's eyes. "Questions?" she said in a low raw voice, "questions? Yeah, I have questions." She stepped close to me. "Why are you standing here while my boy is in a box?" Her voice kept rising, "Why are you alive? Why did Dominick have to die in some filthy jungle a million miles from home? What did he ever do to deserve that? Answer me that, if you can."

A man I took to be Dominick's father rescued me. He put his arm around the shattered woman and guided her back into the house. When he came back, he was accompanied by a young man tricked out in full biker leathers. "I'm Stan Dombroski, Dom's father," he said and turned to the biker, "and this is Dominick's brother, Jerry." The two men stepped out and closed the door behind them. "Please forgive my wife. Dom's death hit her hard."

I shook Mr. Dombrowski's hand, told my lies, and headed back down the walk.

The biker followed me. "Hey, bro, we really appreciate you coming here. Mom's still cut up about it, but we do want to know how it was." He hesitated, "Dom was okay at the end?"

"Yeah, he was okay."

"That's good. Mom and Dad need to know that. Look, you want to get a drink somewhere?"

Yeah, I needed a drink, a strong drink. Jerry and I found ourselves at the bar of a little gin mill staring at each other in the back bar mirror. I ordered a shot and a beer and listened to his questions. He seemed to want the truth so I admitted that Dom had died quickly, but painfully, and was neither liked nor disliked by the rest of the platoon. He was an FNG, a fucking new guy. No one bothered with FNG's until they'd shown that they weren't unlucky.

"And, my brother was unlucky?" he asked.

"Yeah."

"You were lucky." It was half statement and half question.

"Maybe. We'll see."

As the evening wore on, the place filled up, voices got louder and the laughter got shrill. Some idiot overheard us talking about Dom being killed overseas and made a comment about fighting in a "stupid fucking war to save one set of gooks from another." Jerry decked him. One of the idiot's friends went for Jerry. I kicked his knee joint sideways before he could land a blow. The rest of the patrons seemed poised to join in – not on our side – while Jerry and I started thinking about rapid retreat. Order was restored – and our asses saved – by the bartender waving a cut-down baseball bat and yelling at us to get the fuck out. We left.

We ended the evening at the clubhouse of the Misfits Motorcycle Club with a dozen members, a clutch of girls and oceans of booze. Jerry introduced me by yelling out, "Hey, this is Blade. He was a friend of my brother's in Viet Nam. Killed a gook with his knife. He's a jarhead, but don't hold that against him." There was a general mumble of welcome, then everyone went back to doing whatever they'd been doing. My kind of people.

"Killed a gook with a knife?" the guy behind the bar asked. "How'd that happen?"

"You know, it was an accident – could have happened to anybody. I was just walking along in the jungle minding my own business and tripped on a vine or something and stuck that K-Bar into his belly." The guy started laughing. I continued, "I apologized and everything, but he went and died anyway."

He laughed some more and reached across the bar to shake my hand, "Blade, I'm Tommy. I'm kind of in charge of this outfit. Where were you stationed? I was in the Delta"

"Eye Corps, then, later in Saigon."

"Saigon?" his smile went all the way to his eyebrows. "Is that where this knife accident occurred?"

"No, I would have more likely stuck a Frenchman there."

He left me to serve someone further down the bar. Just mentioning that place started it. I could feel the current pulling me back to the heat and killing, pulling hard. It wanted me back. For a moment, boisterous men's voices and fog of cigarette smoke were contained in a sandbagged shack nine thousand miles away. Dombrowski and the other FNG's were on one side of the room trying to look tough. My side ignored them and quietly committed themselves to serious drinking. The unmistakable thunder of a Harley outside gave me an anchor to drag myself back – there were no sounds like that over there. Slowly Dombroski and the FNG's faded, replaced by men with wild hair and leather vests.

They tell you that readjustment to civilian life takes time. No one was very specific about how much time – or how hard it would be or how excluded you would feel. I loathed Viet Nam with every atom of my being. If someone offered me a chance to nuke the whole place, North and South, I would have no difficulty pushing the button. Cleansing that horror with fire might get rid of the dreams.

Tommy came back up the bar. "How long have you been back in the World?"

"Depends on how you count. I was discharged six months ago."

"But?"

"I didn't make as easy an adjustment to civilian life as expected," I said, mimicking the first shrink I had.

"I think we all have had some, what do they call them? *Adjustment difficulties.*" Tommy took a shot with me. "Guess I expected people would still like me when I got home," he said.

"And they didn't?" I needed to joke a little, "Such a fine, upstanding citizens as yourself?"

"Go figure, huh?" He paused for a minute, "they just fucking ignored me, man. Like nothing had happened. Like I'd been in Omaha or someplace on a job. It really pissed me off."

My turn to share. "I had some trouble in San Francisco and had to take some time in the hospital. I beat up a college kid and they were going to charge me with aggravated assault. The cops and the judge liked me – or didn't like the long-haired freak I beat up – and sentenced me to ninety days counseling at the VA for an attitude adjustment."

"Did you hurt him bad?"

"Nah." I truly couldn't remember. "But the little shit was quick enough to go to the cops."

"Where you from?"

"New Hampshire, but I'm never going back."

"You like California, huh?"

"What's not to like. I'm just waiting for Frankie and Annette to show up – actually, just Annette. Frankie can take a hike."

"Fucking-A right! You working?"

"Disability right now, but I gotta find something pretty soon."

"Why don't you crash with me and my old lady while you get settled? Maybe you can find a place near where Annette lives."

The VA counselor had told me that she thought I was wrestling with feelings of guilt. According to her, the best solution would be to make amends – as if I could go back over to that fucking hole and look up the families of the men I killed and say I'm really sorry about your husband or son or brother – or daughter. They were equal opportunity fighters. This, of course, assumed that I hadn't killed the families too.

Even after I was released from the hospital, it was nothing for me to walk through the door of a 7-Eleven and spend a split second into a hooch full of VC soldiers before I could jam those visions back in their box.

I knew it wanted me back and was waiting to crush me into jelly and spread me over that diseased ground. Sometimes just letting go and going back over there was both terrifying and welcoming. If I gave up, I'd never have to worry about making sense of the world again – everything would be easy.

Those feelings still scare me more than the visions of the dead or my longing to be with Phoung.

The visit to the Dombrowski's was an attempt to come to terms (the counselor's words) with the war. He was the only marine who'd actually died with just me there and she thought seeing his family might make things better somehow. Maybe keep me from slipping away, slipping back.

The members of Jerry's club were easy for me to be with. They understood where I'd been and what I'd done and accepted it – even offered respect without the phony "thank you for your service" bullshit. I was comfortable hanging around with them. Somewhere among the beer, the stories and the horseplay I was invited to join the club – I'd already passed my initiation in the bar earlier. After many shots washed down with many beers, everything was possible. I agreed. Nobody seemed to care that I didn't have a motorcycle and wouldn't know how to ride it if I did. There were even a couple of boozy offers to start driver ed immediately.

Phoung's gentle shaking woke me. Shit! I'd fallen asleep. Damn, damn, damn! It was dawn and I was AWOL. My gear had to be somewhere in the hooch, but I couldn't remember where – I needed to saddle up and had to get my ass back to camp pronto! Time in the brig was a certainty, Christ, maybe even court martial. Man, I am in deep shit! Phoung said something, but I didn't understand her. Sometimes her Vietnamese is too idiomatic for me – especially when I'm not at my best.

"You okay, man?" Wow, her English had really improved. "You really scared me. You want coffee or something 'cuz we got some going." Then Phoung's hooch dissolved into a big room with men and women sprawled here and there. I smelled coffee, not sweat and nightsoil. What the hell?

"Phoung, những gì đang xảy ra?" But she couldn't tell me what was happening because her soft round face dissolved into a longer, paler, blue-eyed one. Her clothes changed too. Instead of a rough grey jacket and pants, she was wearing a bright flowered shift and red and yellow beads.

The hippie chick reached for me, her forehead knotted with concern. "I don't understand you, man. *Foon nung gee*…what's that mean?" Her face was framed by straight blonde hair. And I was back.

"Yeah, coffee would be good." I looked around some more "Bathroom?"

"Over there, man," she said pointing. "You sure you're okay?"

I staggered off to complete the resurrection waving away the girl's offer to help. The inside of Phoung's hooch and the Misfits' clubhouse merged and flowed, but I was able to navigate the trail to the bathroom. If I keep going back there like this…I won't. I won't go back. I don't want to see it again. The Bullet can find me here just as easily.

Southern California had always been my dream. As I told Tommy, it was the land of beach parties with Frankie and Annette, sun and simple problems with easy solutions. I'd learn to surf, hang out with Annette and Moondoggy, and drive a cool hot rod. Well, I'd sort of made it. The crappy little apartment I moved into from Tommy's place was at least fifty miles from the beach, but maybe riding with an outlaw biker gang was as good as driving a hot rod. Still waiting for Annette though...

I got a real job. My eight months wrestling with an IBM 7090 in Saigon gave me what they call a marketable skill – there weren't very many people in 1971 who knew anything about computers.

After I recovered from the ministrations of the She-Demon in Viet Nam, my partial disability blocked my return to an infantry unit. The Marine Corps apparently figured that I still owed them six or seven months in country and ordered me to Naval Intelligence. At that time all of the intelligence services were desperate for Americans who could speak Vietnamese – I qualified – barely

I remember sitting in the waiting area of an unmarked office in Saigon. The collar of my service uniform chafed and the whole outfit smelled funny after being stored for months. Rotting utilities and a boonie cover was the preferred apparel for most of my time in Viet Nam. When I was released from the hospital in Okinawa, I was handed a travel chit and ordered to report to a Commander James E. Watson, Naval Intelligence, Saigon.

Still in country, but better than out in the puckerbrush. I didn't want to go back there anyway. Even here in an air-conditioned office with carpets and typewriters and office-type sailors scurrying to and fro, Phoung kept trying to visit me.

She had a delicacy that she carried with her, even when bent over rice plants in a stinking pond decorated with drifting human turds. If the squad passed her on the march, I could sometimes catch her eye and she would smile, but only with her eyes. But, when she looked back at the young plants, I could see that the corners of her mouth were turned up.

I tried to push the image away before the rest of the film unreeled. That beautiful serene face battered and black…

"Corporal Meecham?" a female yeoman with a file folder was standing over me. "You *are* Corporal Meecham, right?"

I leaped up, still mostly wrestling with the past. "Yes, Ma'am!"

She smiled. "No need to Ma'am me, Corporal. I'm an E-3 same as you. Please come with me, the Commander is ready for you." She escorted me through one of the office doors and announced me, "Corporal Meecham, Commander," and left.

It was a large office by government standards, including a conference table as well as the standard grey steel desk, padded steel chairs and grey four-drawer files. Commander Watson was tall and spare with thinning reddish hair. I'd bet he played basketball at Princeton or wherever, belonged to the right fraternity, and would retire as an Admiral. In other words, he radiated WASP.

"Have a seat, Corporal," he said waving me to one of the chairs in front of his desk. "*Bạn có nói tiếng việt?*" (do you speak Vietnamese?) The Commander was being cute, testing to see if I understood what he had asked.

"*Tôi nói tiếng Việt một chút*" (I speak Vietnamese a little)

"*Tốt, đủ để phỏng vấn một tù nhân?*"(Well enough to interview a prisoner?)

"*Vâng* (Yes) I'm sorry Sir I don't know the word for "commander"

149

"That's fine, Meecham, I believe you can get by in Vietnamese." He leaned back in his chair. "Were you able to learn it from the young girl you befriended in *Ban Hoc*? Or do you have some other connection with the country?"

Befriended, that's an interesting description. A seventeen-year-old girl who began to thaw my dead frozen heart was violated and our baby murdered, because I had *befriended* her. The Commander's face dissolved and reformed as Phoung's, then reverted to that of a normal fifty-year old naval officer

He looked at the file on his desk. "How much do you know about the whole Combined Action Program – not just the village garrisons?"

"My squad was assigned to *Ban Noc* as part of CAP. Our mission was to keep our area of operations clear of VC."

Yeah, we cleared out the VC…right up until they decided to clear us out. The *cô quỷ* , the She-Demon, appeared before me, arrogant and sure of herself. "You will suffer for your sins, marine meek-am – and I will rejoice." She pointed back to the clearing. "Look what awaits…"

No, no, no! You're dead and the battle is over. I sweated to see her face as it looked with the hole in her forehead – that's how you ended, *cô quỷ*. It's over. Everything is over…now.

The commander droned on about the finer points of CAP.

"It's not just protecting the villages from the Viet Cong recruiters and tax collectors," he said, "We have to also identify and neutralize the VC cadres in the villages so they can't grow back. The Program relies on The Regional and Popular Forces to round up suspected VC cadres and bring them in for interrogation. The prisoners are then either returned to their villages or imprisoned by the Vietnamese government."

"Yes, Sir." The Ruff-Puff's were the paramilitary forces charged with local defense. Generally poorly armed and untrained, even ARVN saw them as gangsters.

The Commander continued "We're having a tough time with the language barrier, Corporal, and we're hoping that American servicemen who speak Vietnamese can help us." He looked at me expecting a comment.

There was no way in the world that a marine corporal should point out to a full commander in the US Navy the flaw in the elegant system he had outlined – it was based on bullshit and he certainly knew it. The Ruff-Puff's were nothing more than criminal gangs dominated by minority *Nung*, who ran an extortion and protection racket under the guise of searching out communist cadres. They beat up and abducted villagers without evidence then ransomed them back to their families. Those who couldn't or wouldn't pay ended up in the interrogation center or dead in the tall grass along the route.

The problem wasn't the language barrier. The problem was the whole fucking country was corrupt. Everyone was looking for an angle to shake the American money tree – "you want VC, Boss, we give you all kinda VC."

"So, what do you think, Corporal, will you finish out your time in country with us?"

What a fucking idiot. He didn't have to sell me. I didn't have a choice. We follow orders.

In this way, I became part of Naval Intelligence. There were maybe a dozen of us, mostly guys whose parents spoke Vietnamese with a leavening of those of us who'd learned enough over here to pretend we spoke the language.

They gave me a temporary assignment assisting with the set up the new computer system that would make storing and retrieving the information accumulated on suspected VC cadres faster and more accurate...as if bullshit carried out to three decimal places would somehow be more valuable than simple bullshit.

The guys IBM sent were next to useless – once the machine was wired up and passed its diagnostics, they went back to Tokyo. No one in the Navy knew anything, so a couple of us took advantage of the air conditioning and started reading the manuals that came with the machines. It didn't take long for us to light the big box up and start playing around. Two enlisted sailors and I became the computer team. That computer kept me in a nice air-conditioned office and out of any interrogation cells for the rest of my tour. Then I came back to the world.

Now I had a real job that would pay the rent on my crappy apartment and my employer didn't care what I looked like when I came to work. Delta Systems did the DP for small banks and other companies that couldn't afford their own computers. They were desperate for anyone who had computer experience – they had a couple of kids they hired out of high school because they'd been fooling around with Radio Shack TRS-80's. My desire for third shift moved me right to the top of the hiring list. Their enthusiasm didn't extend to movie-star pay, but it was better than anything else I was qualified for.

Third shift was perfect for me. That's when we ran the systems for banks to get them updated information for the next morning. It was also happily short of people wandering around looking for chit-chat. After my time in Viet Nam, I just couldn't get interested in the things that people talked about. They acted like they were immortal, forever chasing after bigger houses, fancier cars or more acclaim. I wanted to grab them by the shirt front and shake them, "you're going to *die,* you stupid fuck. Is *this* what your life is about?"

At least, the Misfits were honest about not giving a shit about anything. I used my mustering-out pay to buy a '67 Harley Davidson shovel head that someone had begun to chop then lost interest. Jerry, who learned mechanics in the Air Force – the sissy – helped me clean it up, strip off the crap and rake it. He and most of the rest of the club took turns teaching me to ride and laughing at my clumsiness. In Southern California, the roads and the weather made riding an everyday thing. When I was riding, I had wings.

The MC gave me a home among a group of men who didn't give a shit about the conventions and restrictions of the straight world. We followed our own code. We respected each other, never asked for anything more than to be left alone to ride and party. I let my hair grow, stopped shaving, drank and fought, and partied with the girls who hung around the club.

DJ and Scope forced me to get a tattoo. "I'm tired of looking at those butt-ugly scars on your arm. You gotta either wear long sleeves or do something about it," was DJ's diplomatic presentation of the problem. "Doesn't the VA have some kind of program or something? It scares the chicks, man."

"You're full of shit, DJ, my scars aren't as ugly as your face, and you do alright." And, he did have incredible success with women.

"If you won't do plastic surgery, at least get a tattoo to cover them up."

He started a movement in the MC to push me into getting tattooed and to decide what tattoo would be best. When I finally agreed – why not – I was shown the winning entry.

"There is no fucking way I'm going to have a gaping wound dripping blood on my arm or a drawing of a knife carving the word Blade into my skin. You people are sick."

We settled on the USMC emblem for the entrance wound and a dragon around my arm where the stick came out by my elbow. Getting the first one hurt so damn much that I left the exit scar as it was.

Things went along pretty well for a while. My life wasn't exactly Ozzie and Harriet, but I had my little routine, actually got a couple of raises at work and had some people to be with. If I drank enough and rode fast enough and made it with enough empty-headed chicks, I could forget for minutes at a time the weight of the bodies I carried.

My wallow in sin and sloth ended in early 1972. President Nixon began his second term with a promise of peace with honor, by which he meant betray your allies and bug the fuck out. And the Body Counters Motorcycle Club began to crowd us. I don't know if the two events are connected except that they both pissed me off.

The Counters were probably the largest and certainly the best known one-percent motorcycle club on the West Coast. They even claimed to be the club that picked up on a statement by the Motorcycle Manufacturers Association that said that "...99% of all motorcyclists are law-abiding citizens..." and emblazoned a bright yellow 1% badge on their colors.

The mother chapter just outside of Oakland had been featured in a dozen national magazines – usually to titillate the civilians with tales of violence and grotesque rituals. They claimed more than two dozen chapters across the country and were expanding southward.

We were aware of groups of Body Counters riding around in the local area, but they gave us enough room to keep the peace – until Crow got beaten half to death.

Johnny C., whose last name was a string of unpronounceable consonants, called from the hospital and I took the call, "The motherfuckers jumped us!" he snarled. "Now Crow in is surgery. Sonofabitch hit him with a piece of pipe."

"What? Where are you?"

"I'm in the emergency room with two cops. They took the cuffs off so's I could call. Get some guys down here, man. Crow's in a really bad way, man. Come down here, okay?"

"Johnny, we'll be there. What happened? What's with the cops?"

"I gotta go, man,' and he hung up.

I turned to the expectant faces. "Where's Tommy?"

"He's out back with his lady."

"Get him…now!"

Tommy took control, called and gave our lawyer a heads-up, then led us to the hospital. Hospital security started to freak out when we showed up. The two city cops at the front desk nervously fingered their side arms as they approached our group – a dozen wild-looking men in black leather.

Tommy, ever the diplomat, stepped forward. "Officers, we understand that a friend of ours had been seriously injured. We're here to see what we can do for him." That smooth, highly-educated voice was oil on the water. And, since we hadn't eaten any children or raped anyone since we arrived, everyone calmed down.

The cops were shoulder-to-shoulder in front of us, still looking for the slightest sign of trouble. "We have one of your members in custody and another is in surgery. One of you can come over and speak to the nurses, the rest sit down over there," nodding toward an area remote from everyone else. Tommy waved us over and we went like good little boys, while Tommy walked off with the cops.

I watched Tommy confer with the medical staff, then with the cops, then with Johnny C. Everyone in the Emergency Room heard Johnny's response to whatever Tommy said. "What the fuck? We didn't do anything. They jumped us. And, they're gonna pay…." Tommy got him settled down and came over to us.

"Okay, Crow's got a fractured skull – the doctor called it a depressed fracture that required them to drill some holes in his head to lower the pressure on his brain. That's what they're doing now."

"Christ! They better be sure no brains leak out – Crow ain't got much to start with," someone said.

Tommy smiled and continued, "It's going to take a while so we don't all need to sit here and scare the people. Johnny's in cuffs because he resisted arrest. As soon as he's checked out, the cops are taking him in."

"Who did this? Have the cops got them, too?"

"Yeah, they've got three Body Counters over at our Lady of Mercy being patched up. The cops were smart enough not to put us all in the same emergency room. Crow needed surgery right away so we're here and the Counters are over at Mercy.

"But, what happened?" I asked Tommy, "what the hell happened?"

"Not sure. Johnny says they were jumped. The Counters claim our guys attacked them. We'll figure it out. I've called Ferris and told him to meet me at the station to make sure Johnny gets out as soon as possible. Blade, you and DJ stay here until we know what's up with Crow. Everyone else, back to the clubhouse. We'll talk later."

Everyone stood to take on their assignments. Tommy stopped us, "From now on, no one rides alone. Everyone should have another member watching his six."

Crow's operation was successful although he had to face months of rehabilitation. Everyone calmed down a little but the truce didn't last and provocations continued.

My experience was typical. On my way through town, I noticed half a dozen choppers lined up in the lot of the local hamburger joint. By the time I was half a mile down the road, they came roaring up behind me, moving fast and weaving in and out of traffic.

It was nine o'clock in the morning, traffic was heavy and I was tired from working a full shift so I decided to give them bragging rights for passing me. I eased over to the right a little and waited. The first pair passed then swerved in making me grab the brakes to avoid a crash. The next guy past stuck out his right foot trying to kick my front fork. He missed but braked hard after swinging into my lane forcing me to slow way down. The Counters boxed me in and tried to force me toward the shoulder. The outside rider was actually leaning against me!

I knew that hitting the loose gravel on the road shoulder would send me ass over teakettle without a hope of recovery. I downshifted and braked, my outside rider slowed with me. I jumped on the throttle and blasted through the hole that opened up in front of us, taking the bike all the way to the red line in third gear. I hit fourth at about eighty-five and kept the wick turned up until I found a place to turn off and lose them.

When I described it to the other members, DJ suggested, "Would be a good way to cause a fatal motorcycle accident, wouldn't it?"

"You mean like the one that killed Mac a couple of weeks ago?" asked Scope.

Mac was a good rider and crashed on the Hilltop Road in broad daylight stone-cold sober. The Highway Patrol decided he was going too fast through one of the tight corners, ran off the road and hit some boulders and a tree. They also felt compelled to point out that he wasn't wearing a helmet – like that would have made a difference.

Johnny C was up for a raid. "Why don't we mount the heads of one or two of those fuckers on sticks and plant them in the parking lot of that bar they like so much?"

"Hey, bro, what do you think would happen then? We hit them, they hit us and nothing changes." Tommy made palm-down cooling gestures, "Let's just be careful and give them a chance to act like men, huh?"

Tommy and Calvin arranged to meet with the leaders of the local Body Counters group.

"When we walked in there, man, there was, like, twenty of them. The whole fucking bar was full of Counters – we didn't even have a place to sit." Calvin was outraged by the lack of respect.

Tommy agreed, "They pretty much expected us to kiss their asses and ask politely if we could ride on their roads." He stopped for a minute and smiled, "then Calvin went nuts."

"I didn't go nuts. I was getting some leverage."

Tommy turned to the group, "Here we are, all these bad dudes staring at us. Chuckie Boy is just leaning back with a beer smiling, and Calvin, here, is standing there like Big Chief I Don't Give A Damn." Tommy imitated Calvin standing up to his full six-foot-four, arms crossed over his chest. "He's looking down like he just noticed a turd on the floor.

"I was looking at Chuckie Boy," said Calvin. "Pretty much the same thing."

"Then, this dipshit unfolds his arms and he's holding an Army .45 automatic in each hand. He walks over to Chuckie and tells him…"

"I told him he was a dead man, and that I could kill most of the rest of his men before they got me." Calvin's level tone hinted that he really didn't give a damn if it went that way. "Of course, you were just a little lamb. Pulling out that goddamned dog."

Tommy had a sawed off double-barreled shotgun that, with the stock cut down to just a pistol grip, couldn't be more than a foot long. The spread of shot would be like setting off a Claymore mine. He called it his "dog", a play on the British criminal nickname, whippet. "You didn't think I believed Chuckie's bullshit about a truce, did you?" Everyone laughed.

"I told Chuckie that we would stay out of their way, and they could have the whole territory except our little area from Durham back to Springfield and down to St. Jerome. Everywhere else, they could do whatever gangster shit they liked. Out in the open, each group would leave the other alone."

Johnny C. and some of the others weren't happy with the diplomatic solution. "We're giving them all of fucking Southern California – who the fuck do they think are anyway?" Johnny bellowed. "Why surrender to these bastards?

"They *think* they're the guys with the most men and the biggest need. They *think* they're the ones who are willing to kill to get what they want. They *think* they're the ones who will wipe us out, if we don't arrange some kind of truce," Tommy looked hard at Johnny C. "I love this club enough to save it and I don't give a shit if that hurts your pride."

Happy or otherwise, everyone respected Tommy's decision. It did keep a lid on things for a while. We'd given them a free pass to the border to move their drugs. As Calvin put it, "If they want to move that shit up and down the coast, why do we care? Their clubs live and die with drugs. We don't and we're not going to start. So why get people killed?"

I was in the clubhouse bar about eight o'clock in the morning a few days after the big powwow, gearing down after a rough night at work. A blonde girl plumped herself down on the stool next to me. "Nice breakfast" she said motioning to the shot and beer in front of me." She turned to face me and to give me a two-count to admire unconstrained breasts in a too-tight tee shirt, then continued. "Did you hear that the Counters set up a chapter over near Calli? They're calling themselves Body Counters SoCal with a lower rocker and everything."

"No, I didn't hear that," I answered, still mostly focused on the tee shirt, "but that's like seventy miles away. It's part of the deal." I tossed back the shot and took a sip of my beer. "So, who are you and how do you know all this?"

"I know all kinds of things." Her smile contained all of the ancient wisdom of womankind. She reached over and shook a Kool out of my pack. "I'm Aster, you know, like the flower" She held the cigarette between her lips and turned to me expecting a light. I figured that if she could help herself to a cigarette, she could help herself to my lighter lying beside the pack.

"You were a marine, huh?" she asked, noting birdie on the ball emblem engraved into the Zippo's face. "Like really tough guys, stone killers and all? Were you in Viet Nam?"

I nodded.

"You shoot anyone?"

"Probably." My standard answer.

"What does that mean? Did you or didn't you?" She took a deep drag, "I need to know who I'm dealing with here." Then she laughed, "Don't want to get hurt, you know." I probably used that tone of invulnerability once, too.

"I don't know that you're dealing with me, Aster-like-the-flower. I certainly wouldn't want to cause you any pain."

She cocked her head and squinted at me, "Wait a minute, you're the one they call Blade, right? Killed guys with a knife?"

"Yes and no. One guy. And, it was dumb luck."

"Tell me about it."

"No"

She drew her head back frowning. "Okay, try this. What the hell happened to give you that scar?" She pointed to the white puckered skin under my tat. "Can you tell me about that?"

"No."

"No?" she pouted, then leaned towards me, "don't you like me?"

"I like you fine, but there's nothing from over there that you need to know about. Why don't you tell me about yourself," I said, "like what's your real name."

"The name on my birth certificate is Astrid, but it isn't me. It's like some tight-assed Nazi bitch, you know?" She took another drag on her cigarette. "I have this really strong connection with Nature. Like, we're all part of the larger Universe." She'd swallowed – or at least spouted – the whole flower child credo. She seemed to believe most of it. "If we'd just love one another, we wouldn't need marines to fight wars and you can spend all your time making love to me," she said. Well, hell, people have to believe something.

We latched on to each other and spent most of our free time together. She moved into my place, rode with me when we went out with the club. She became identified as "Blade's old lady", which gave her more status around the club than just one of the girls hanging around.

Our lives were pretty simple. We went to work – she had a job at a junk jewelry place in town – and then we hung out with the MC. She smoked dope and I drank. Sex was simple and conversations minimal.

It was inevitable that we would start expecting more from ourselves and each other.

"Why the fuck can't you wash a dish once in a while?" Maybe it was the service or a reaction to my mother's cavalier approach to housework, but dirty dishes and sticky floors drive me nuts.

"What's your problem, man?"

"My problem, *man*, is the pile of filthy damn dishes providing a nest for bugs in our sink, the open loaf of bread on the table, the crap piled everywhere. We're living in a pig sty! And, you apparently don't mind. That's what's bugging me, *man*."

"Bugs gotta eat, too, ya know."

"Not in my house." I put away the bread and threw away the empty peanut butter jar – along with the ant colony living in it. Storming around the kitchen, heaving shit into plastic garbage bags, I managed to find the tops of the counters and table. After a trip to the dumpster, I attacked the dishes. "I don't understand how anyone can be near anything like this," I was muttering to myself, half hoping she'd hear me and take notice. "Damnit!" a bunch of roaches scuttled out from under a plate. Disgusting creatures.

Bugs. There were so many bugs over there – creeping and crawling and sneaking into places they shouldn't, spreading who knows what kinds of diseases. That place was like an incubator for big, swarming, shit-eating bugs – extra legs, extra eyes, big sharp jaws, every conceivable deformity. I could feel them crawling...

"Baby, you're so upset. Chill out."

Aster's hands on my shoulders felt like giant crawling...something. I twisted away.

"Easy, man, I didn't mean to surprise you. Everything's cool. Just relax." She put her arms around my neck and pulled me down into a kiss. At least she hadn't gone completely hippie and given up bathing. She rested her head against my chest. "You went away for a minute, didn't you? Back to Viet Nam again, huh?"

"Yeah, I guess. I..."

"Shssh." She put her fingers on my lips. "Come with me."

She led me into the bedroom. "Take your clothes off and lie down...nice try...face down." She straddled my butt and expertly massaged my neck and shoulders. "You're back home, Baby, with me now. You don't have to worry about what you did, or what they did – it's over, you're home. Nothing to be afraid of. You're safe with me."

My heartrate slowed, I could feel the tension drain away under her fingers. As I relaxed the obvious thoughts arose. I turned over and tried to pull her granny dress up over her head, but she stopped me.

"Get some rest, man. We can do that later. Right now you need to get all the way back into the world. Maybe, you'd let me hold you for a little while?"

I slept. My only dreams of that place were pretty ones of being with Phuong, listening to her laugh at my butchered pronunciation and trying to understand the quiet, accepting virtues of a culture thousands of years older than my own. When I awoke, the apartment was just as I'd left it – Aster hadn't transformed into a hausfrau while I was asleep. I'd have to be satisfied with her affection and willingness to pull me back from the edge.

We learned that discussion of war, peace, love, responsibility, cleanliness and all other serious topics just led to nasty fights – she was much more intelligent than her naïve philosophy indicated and generally argued me into frustrated silence. Sometimes the fights ended up as rough foreplay and sometimes as hard-shelled silence.

The breaking point was the MC's response to the Counters. When I told her about Calvin and Tommy's summit meeting, which I thought was funny. She was furious.

"That's exactly the kind of macho bullshit that keeps wars going – some idiot, in this case Calvin, showing how big his dick is instead of trying to find a solution," she snarled.

"But Tommy made a good offer," I protested.

"Sure, after both he and Calvin had threatened them with guns – how would you feel if you went into a peace conference and the other side pulled guns?"

"That's really what they did by having so many guys there…"

"No excuse. Look at Gandhi, for God's sake! Lying down in front of tanks. That's how you solve problems without violence."

"No, that's how you get your ass run over unless you just happen to pick and opponent who cares about the niceties – like the Brits."

"Watch me being passive and non-violent. I agree with you completely, Dear."

"Fuck you!"

"Don't think so, big guy."

####

Johnny C. wasn't a big admirer of the Gandhi approach or of Tommy's truce. He staged a one-man raid on the bar the Body Counters used as a headquarters. He shot a couple of Counters, got shot himself and ended up charged with two counts of attempted murder.

After that, the cops rousted us every couple of weeks. They'd crash in, line everybody up and check identification – that was one of their favorites.

At that time, California was the prime destination for runaways. The cops checking ID's would almost always turn up a runaway girl or two, who were summarily sent back to Iowa or wherever. Then they'd test to see if we'd been serving alcohol to minors. Then they'd tear the place apart looking for drugs or weapons. Anyone who normally carried a gun or a knife left it with his bike – they never searched the motorcycles. On the road, we couldn't pass a cop without getting pulled over on some pretext. The law enforcement tactic was to make life so miserable that we'd just give up and go away, I guess.

We assumed that the Body Counters were getting the same treatment but it didn't stop them from coming after any Misfit they saw. Riding a chopper became hazardous to your health – even if you weren't part of any club.

The pressure from the cops was bad enough, but to be shot at for no reason other than you weren't wearing the right colors was new to us.

Worst of all, we were losing. A couple of our guys were in hospital and Johnny C. was in jail. Yuma had to go on the run after he shot and killed a Counter in a gunfight. The Misfits had always been a small club and had never recruited or attempted to expand.

As Tommy often said, "we don't want to let any more assholes in – with you guys our asshole quota is filled."

The Body Counters had the growth philosophy of a cancer cell and easily replaced members killed, wounded or incarcerated – it was sort of their point of pride.

Most of us now changed into civilian clothes and took our cars to work instead of our bikes so we'd be sure to get there without any trouble. I was still in civvies talking with Tommy about what in the hell we could do to end this shit, when Aster motioned me over.

"I just got some news, Blade." She took a deep breath then blurted out, "I'm going to have a baby!" She was all smiles.

"What? A baby?" If she'd hit me with a brick, I couldn't have been more stunned. "Mine?"

"Of course, asshole. And I'm moving up north to a cool commune away from all this. It's a place where I can raise him to be one with Nature and free of all the shit that kids are indoctrinated with." She kissed me on the cheek and headed for the door.

"Wait a minute! 'I'm going to have your baby – see ya'?" I started toward her, "Don't I get anything to say about this?"

"No." And she was gone.

I got a letter from her some time later postmarked San Francisco and forwarded from our old address. She said that she and Carson – that's what she named the baby boy – were attempting to live in peace and harmony with the All. If I felt like it, I could send money to a post office box. I sent five hundred dollars, but the check was never cashed.

Then the bastards firebombed the clubhouse. We thought we were safe there. We never put out sentries or anything like that –

hell, we weren't really at war. There were the usual eight or ten of us inside along with a gathering of hangers on and groupie-type girls, maybe twenty people in total, when the front door blew in. A girl standing at the bar was drenched with burning gas, screaming and thrashing. A second bomb came through the open door and engulfed half the bar.

While we were trying to put people out and save the building, a dozen gunshots ripped through the windows, followed by the roar of departing motorcycles. Two members and some suburbanite's daughter died.

The Misfits were officially dissolved four days later. The VFW let us use their place for our final meeting. Tommy opened the floor to the remaining members saying, "I don't see any way for us to keep going. They're fucking criminals and we're not. I don't want any more killing. All we ever wanted was to be free. Now good people, innocent people have died. I'm done." He looked around the group for anyone who would step forward and challenge him. No one did. We were beaten. The Body Counters wanted to own Southern California all the way to the Mexican border and were willing to kill all of us to get it. We weren't willing to kill all of them.

There was, however, the issue of our honor. The last official order of business for the Misfits MC was to avenge our dead. "We'll draw lots to see which two of us will have the jobs of punishing the fucking Body Counters SoCal." He counted out eleven marbles, nine white and two black, -- probably from his son's Chinese checkers game – and put them into an old helmet. We each drew one blind, then opened our hands simultaneously. Scope and I were holding black marbles.

"Blade, Scope, you know what you have to do."

Tommy looked around the group. "Okay, men, take off your colors and put them away with your other trophies – you've worn

167

them with honor." His voice grew rougher. "The Misfits Motorcycle Club is hereby dissolved.

Scope was fearless. He wore thick ugly glasses with an elastic strap holding them on "...so he could see who he was hitting..." So I was floored when he asked Tommy, "Are you sure about this revenge stuff, man? They're for sure going to come back at us whether we're wearing colors or not. Some of these guys have families and stuff. Maybe the best thing is just to let it go."

DJ, who had a wife and two kids, snapped, "Don't use me as an excuse for not doing what has to be done, Scope. We'll take care of whatever happens afterwards."

Tommy checked the nodding heads around the table. "Okay," he said, "We agree these bastards have earned it. Scope, Blade, good hunting!" Scope got up and headed for the door. I hurried after him.

We stood together outside the hall. Scope pointed out another thing to consider. "When this started the cops didn't care if we killed each other as long as no one else got hurt. Hell, with the riots, hard hats beating up demonstrators, hippies stoned out of their gourds, and the blacks burning down whole neighborhoods, no one missed the occasional biker. There's too many bodies now. The Counters might kill us, but the cops will put us in a little box for the rest of our lives – we don't want that, bro."

"It's just one more obstacle to get past, Man. Adapt, Improvise and Overcome, right?" I answered. "Let's just do what we know how to do and figure the rest out afterwards."

"Adapt, Improvise and Overcome...fucking jarheads" was Scope's only comment.

I didn't believe that anyone would miss my target, Charles L. "Chuckie Boy" Joseph the President of Body Counters SoCal.

Rather than a biker, he had proven himself to be a sadistic psychopath who happened to ride a motorcycle. He rose in the mother chapter up north by scaring the shit out of the other members and devising ever more depraved events to shock and horrify civilians and bond the club members to each other.

His signature was one of those WWI trench knives with spiked brass knuckles as a grip. He kept the knucks polished like they were the family silver and searched for chances to use them. One of the stories circulating in San Francisco was that Chuckie got two of his guys to hold a hooker down while he beat her ass to hamburger with the spiked knuckles, then fucked her. This is the guy that the Counters sent to establish their MC down here.

Scope had drawn Chuckie Boy's number-two man called Jazz. He got the nickname from his crank habit. Jazz was jazzed most of the time – twitchy, dangerous and unpredictable. The world would be a better place without either of these two.

"You know, Scope, my boy, what we ought to do is set up a little ambush with an M-60 machine gun and a bag full of hand grenades," I suggested. "Then we just go in afterward and shoot the wounded."

"Great idea! Now just where do you propose we get the M-60?"

"Well, you have to admit that it has some appeal."

"While you ponder how to get all that hugely illegal ordinance, how about we work on a plan to take out our targets that might actually be doable."

"Maybe, instead, I'll locate the new lab that Chuckie and the boys set up. Even if we don't get him, we'd hurt his wallet."

Scope frowned. "What new lab?"

"A brand new meth lab, bro, set up somewhere out in the desert that's taking up a lot of Chuckie Boy's time. Why don't I see if I can track down the actual location and you make sure we have the right equipment to take down the lab and see if you can get an idea of Chuckie and Jazz's movements?"

"How are you going to find this lab?"

"Magic, bro. Trust me."

My old Jeep CJ was right at home riding around in the desert. The girl who had told me about the new lab had been hanging around with Jazz until she got pissed and showed up at our place.

"That sonofabitch handed me off to some other smelly guy like he was donating old clothes." She took a long drag on her cigarette. "I'm not some piece of meat he can just give away. Fucker!"

"Why come here? Didn't you get enough of bikers over there?" I asked. "You have to know that we're just a dinky little club."

"Yeah," she interrupted, "a dinky little club that's got Chuckie Boy and that shit Jazz all cranked up."

"Us?"

"Yeah, they're afraid you guys are going to screw up this new lab they set up."

"What new lab would that be, honey?"

"Out in the desert somewhere. About eight miles from Clifford, he said. Over shit roads. Jazz was bitching that the road beat his ass, but, of course, he *had* to ride that hard-tail bike. He couldn't just take a car or a truck like an intelligent human being."

Another drag, "I can tell you, man, you hit a bump with that thing and it'll kick your ass up between your shoulder blades – 'course *his* seat had springs."

With the general location she gave me, finding the lab might be possible though simple legwork. While there's a whole lot of empty out there, there aren't many roads either. I got a 7.5 minute USGS topo map of the Clifford area and started quartering the area.

Driving around out there gave me a way to avoid facing the truth about the premeditated murders Scope and I had agreed to commit. I'd killed a shitload of people, but this was different. The nasty little demon in my head asked "How? You sat at the edge of the trail waiting for a VC patrol to wander into your field of fire. You cut those guys down by the dozens. What makes killing a fat psychopath and a crank addict so different? It wouldn't be because they're white, would it?" Maybe.

Sand and mesquite flickered and faded into elephant grass and wait-a-minute thorn bushes, then back again. The current swept me toward the heat and the stink of the jungle, toward a world where nothing mattered – where a dead man stalked and killed other men. And I did, day after day, week after week. Until the She-Demon caught me and caged me, beat me and burned me. And in the end, it was she who lost – I didn't win. Weak voices spoke of purpose and debts. "There's no escape," they said. "You can't change what you are or where you're going."

I've always been lucky, and, sure enough, two choppers passed me in a swirl of dust and the blatt of open pipes. Their passing pulled me out of the current and set me ashore back to California. The riders were in Counters colors. The problem with being lucky is the luck can be bad as well as good.

I didn't have any trouble following them, since the land was flat and there were hardly any places to turn off. I kept up with them as well as I could, pushing my poor old Jeep to speeds it hadn't seen in years. I kept going when my quarry turned off, mentally marking the "road" for later exploration.

Scope and I met at McDonald's that evening. "It looks like Chuckie Boy and Jazz are personally overseeing the new lab." Scope said around his Big Mac. "They're spending most of their time out there. Unless we can find the damn lab, they're out of reach right now." He took a sip of his Coke, "and I found just the right equipment to send them, and any of their buddies that happen to be around, straight to hell."

"You need to shine up that equipment, bro, 'cause I have a pretty good idea where they're hiding. After I get off work tomorrow morning, I'm making sure."

"No shit? how'd you do that?"

"Just like always – dumb luck."

After work the next morning, I headed out in the Jeep again. Finding the turnoff wasn't hard. It led me off into real hardscrabble, past the occasional sagging building, sun-beaten with old cars and unidentifiable equipment for company. They were the garrisons in the battle against the desert – and the desert was winning.

After five miles bumping and bashing over the current track, I spotted a turnoff leading up into the hills to the right. The deep grooves of motorcycle tires were the only hint that it wasn't just another abandoned path where a road used to be. It looked like I should explore on foot – there was no telling how far back in the puckerbrush the bikers had gone and I didn't want to surprise them just yet.

I drove past, not wanting to draw attention to myself if they had sentries posted. A half mile past the turn off, my progress was stopped by a deep gully that ran downhill across the road and wound between two little hills below me. Although the track continued on the other side, this was the end for anything that wasn't short-wheelbase and four-wheel drive. Time for some desert hiking.

It wasn't too hard to find the lab. Once I'd shut off the Jeep, I could follow the rattle of a big diesel generator to it. A half hour after leaving the jeep under the lip of the gully, I was looking down at the Body Counters latest meth lab. It wasn't impressive – a beat-up house trailer with an addition built on one end and a roofed area that must have originally been an equipment shed. Now it shaded three dusty Harleys and a battered pick-up truck. Comfortably hidden by the big boulders, I glassed the area with the Nikon binoculars from my pack. Nothing was moving.

The heat began to rise with the sun – my internal debate about how long to sit here was settled by someone moving around the added-on structure. In the binoculars, I could see a guy with a respirator shoved up on his forehead lighting up a cigarette and heading for a shady spot below me. One of the trailer doors slammed open shortly after and two barefooted guys in saggy jeans sauntered a few feet from the trailer and urinated. Morning had broken.

Beneath the beer gut of the shorter of the two men, the unmistakable glint of the brass-knuckled handle of Chuckie Boy's trench knife. I'd never seen Jazz, but the dude next to Chuckie fit his description, tall and skinny with a big beard.

After retreating to the Jeep and heading back, I stopped at big supermarket center about ten miles from where the highway turn off.

From a pay phone outside the market, I checked in with Scope. "I was right and both of our friends are there. Are you ready?"

"As ready as I'll ever be for something like this."

"You want to give it up?" I wasn't sure what answer I was hoping for.

"Can't. Said we'd do it. That's it." Classic Scope. Why use two words when one would do?

We agreed to meet here later that in the evening. The idea was to get into position while it was too hot for anyone to be out frogging around, set up and wait, then hit them just before dawn

I went back to the Jeep, moved it to an unobtrusive spot, and stretched out to sleep for a couple of hours.

Scope's beat-up Chevy 4X4 pulled up alongside my Jeep just as it was getting dark. I grabbed my pack and climbed into the passenger seat beside Scope. "Good to see you, bro. Do we need anything before we head out?" I nodded toward the grocery store.

"Nope," he said. "all I needed was another dummy, and you're here"

"Good, then let's get down to business."

Scope drove while I navigated and described the lab and my thoughts on an approach. After a couple of questions, he was satisfied and we drove on in silence.

"How many?"

"Four," I said, "Chuckie Boy, Jazz, the chemist and one other. From the empties stacked around, it looks like they spend most of their time drinking and watching satellite TV."

"They got electricity?" Scope asked incredulous.

"Sure, got a big old generator hammering away. Makes enough noise to cover the approach of a tank."

"Assholes," he said. "But that's good for us. They'll be drunked up and sleeping by two or three in the morning and we can catch all four of them inside."

"It could be a real bitch going from room to room in a damn trailer. No room to maneuver."

"No reason to go inside at all."

I let that comment slide.

We were in our staging position blocking the track up to the trailer by seven o'clock, got out and started unloading. He reached behind the seat and dragged out a couple of dark green ponchos and handed me one. "It's hot still, but it'll be damn cold in a few hours. These will also break up our outlines if anyone's out nosing around.

He climbed up into the bed of the truck and started moving things around. A long plastic-wrapped package was the first thing he pulled out, followed by a milk crate with half dozen whiskey bottles filled with gasoline. There was a surprise in the first package – two short-barreled 12 gauge shotguns. I was shocked – the guns were old exposed hammer Model 97 Winchesters. They were the kind that had been sold as riot guns to police forces all over the country from the turn of the century until the 1960's. With its short barrel and no hammer interlock, it was called the trench sweeper by our soldiers in WWI. All a doughboy had to do was point it, hold the trigger back and pump the action to empty his six-shot magazine in a single continuous blast. I'd even heard that some of them made it to Viet Nam.

"Where did you get these relics?" I asked. "You sure they won't blow up in our hands?"

"Damn sure, brother," he smiled, "tested them before I came down here. Belonged to my old man. He got them from the prison when they changed over to more humane equipment. Check the dates, they're not as old as you think."

I looked. The one I had in my hands had a manufacture date of 1951 and the other one was 1948. I remember the ads for these shotguns in the back pages of the *American Rifleman* when I was a kid: "Riot guns $29.95 postpaid." The guns looked clean and well maintained and there was no question of their lethality.

Scope looked over and asked, "What are you worried about? They probably weren't fired but a dozen times in thirty years. They're practically new." He opened a second package which contained boxes of double-ought buckshot ammunition and started loading his shotgun. I loaded mine and dumped half a dozen extra shells in each pocket of my jacket. If I needed more than that, I was probably totally screwed anyhow.

An outcrop of rocks about fifty yards from the truck provided cover while we waited. Anyone who tried to enter or leave would have to dismount from their vehicle and get around our pickup on foot exposed to our shotguns.

Scope reached over and retrieved a baby food jar he'd taken from the glove compartment. He opened it and started smearing the black goop on his face. "Soot from my fireplace and Vaseline, dipshit," he said in response to my look, and handed the little jar to me.

He stretched out covered with his poncho. "Give me two hours, then I'll take over." Within minutes his breathing had slowed and his body relaxed in sleep. My old man always said that was the mark of a good field soldier, catch up on your sleep when you can – you can never tell when you'll have to go without.

We alternated two-hour watches. When I spelled him around midnight, Scope shivered, "Jeez, it got cold, didn't it?"

"It'll get worse probably."

At three o'clock, Scope woke me. Time to go. We each carried three Molotov cocktails as well as the guns, as we walked toward the lab. Gunshots sent us diving for cover. Then there was laughter and more gunshots. More laughter. What the hell was going on?

Scope covered me as I moved up to where I could see the trailer, then I waved him up. Chuckie Boy and Jazz were having a middle-of-the-night shooting match, trying to hit beer cans at twenty yards by the light of a dim outside light of the trailer. Drunk.

I turned to Scope, "What the hell is that cannon Chuckie Boy's using?" My words were punctuated by a series of booms that had small pebbles cascading down the cliffs.

"That is a Desert Eagle. A .44 Magnum automatic, guaranteed to deafen you, sprain your wrist and impress your friends." Boom, boom, boom. "His ears will be ringing for weeks, he keeps shooting like that."

Sand sprayed up all around the line of beer cans, but none of them were hit. Jazz wasn't much better. He was using a Glock of some sort and ripped off a dozen rounds hitting one can.

"Maybe we'll get lucky and they'll shoot each other."

"You think we could take them from here?"

Scope shook his head. "It's got to be seventy-five yards. These things spray pellets really wide. Not a sure thing."

"Ain't nothing for sure, brother."

Before we could act on the decision, the two marksmen wandered back to the trailer arguing over who was the worse shot.

It didn't take long for us to figure out why they were hacking around in the middle of the night. About every forty five minutes, the chemist took a cigarette break. He was clearly working the night shift when it was cooler. When I'd seen him in the morning, he must have been wrapping up. The actual lab was in the addition while the trailer was the group's living quarters.

It was five o'clock that morning, the chemist was about due for a cigarette, I signaled Scope to move up to the trailer, then followed him. The addition, sitting up on cement blocks to get it up to the floor level of the trailer, was about twelve feet square, with no windows and a lean-to type metal roof. It had a restaurant-style exhaust fan cut into one of the walls running full blast. There was a door and a set of crude steps at the extreme rear leading down to an open area where they threw their trash and where the chemist took his breaks.

The trailer lived up to every negative stereotype anyone has ever heard. The siding was rusty and peeling away in places; it had had skirts (most were missing), and the cement blocks that served as a foundation were visible. Someone had done a roof repair with a big blue plastic tarp and a couple of old tires. The same three bikes were under the equipment shed roof. A couple of old cars, a washing machine and unidentified junk lined the edges of the beaten down gravel that served as a driveway. The chemical smell was strong enough for me to pick up from here. Real careful, these boys. All of the lights were on.

Scope turned to me, "you want to wait for them to pass out?"

"Fuck no. I'm done waiting."

If they'd taken a little more care building the addition, or were better carpenters, we might have been surprised on our approach. We were halfway across the space when the cursing and shaking of the sticking door warned us that the chemist was coming out. Ignoring the long history of meth labs exploding, he stepped out, stripped off his respirator and lit a cigarette. He had more faith in his exhaust system than I would have had.

Scope nodded at him. I handed him my shotgun and slid along the edge of the building being as quiet as I could. It didn't matter – in addition to the noise of the generator, my target had a set of earbuds in and was humming along with whatever he was listening to.

I pulled the K-Bar out of its sheath and stepped up behind him. My left arm was around his throat and the eight-inch blade shoved up through his kidney and into his lung before he knew I was there. He made a glugging sound and arched back exposing his throat. The knife severed his trachea and right carotid artery. Messy, but certain.

Scope moved up and handed me the two shotguns while he squatted down and fussed with the gasoline-filled whiskey bottles. He stood up, tossed two bottles into the lab through the open door, and moved us away from the little building. Nothing happened. We crouched in the sand expectantly for what seemed like twenty minutes. Suddenly there was a whoosh and the whole damn end of the lab was engulfed in flames.

I lighted one of my cocktails and smashed it against the trailer door farthest from the lab. The roaring fire completely blocked that door, leaving only one possible exit, which Scope was covering. Over the sound of the fires, we could hear crashes and panicked shouts and screams from inside.

The door burst open and two big guys rolled out, stumbling over each other and cursing. Scope opened up with the shotgun clamped against his side, pumping the action continuously until he'd emptied the magazine.

The heavy recoil of the buckshot shells rocked Scope's tall skinny frame back causing him to rock forward in rhythm, dancing with the gun. The bright white spray of muzzle flash strobed my view of the effect of Scope's fire. It was not poetic – the two men basically came apart. The coroner was going to have his work cut out just trying to figure out how many people that pile represented.

I was so mesmerized by Scope's work, that I almost forgot my own assignment. I could hear someone still thrashing around and screaming for help at my end of the trailer. The screams became louder and more agonized. I had no interest in rescuing whoever was in there but took pity on him and emptied my shotgun through the door and side of the trailer. The screaming stopped.

Out of the corner of my eye, I saw Scope ease up to the open door in front of him and heave his last firebomb in. When it went off the windows of the trailer blew out and the whole structure dissolved in flames. I didn't hear any more noises from inside.

We heaved the body of the chemist as close to the back door as possible and smashed my last cocktail against the wall there. "Probably won't fool anyone, but meth labs do explode," I said as we stood watching the inferno.

I fell under a glamour. The trailer in the desert and hooches in a jungle clearing merged in front of me. It was all the same, the heat, the roar of the flames, the roast pork smell of burning bodies and the muscle memory of the recoil from a high-powered weapon. The fumes bit my nose and throat – VC and outlaw bikers look and smell the same when in a pyre like this.

I wasn't certain where I was or of today's truth. Is this my life? I have proven myself an effective killing automaton – again. To what end?

We stood there floating in our own visions until the trailer collapsed breaking the spell. Scope turned to me, "Let's get the fuck out of Dodge, bro."

We left.

PUCKERBRUSH PAGE
What and where is Puckerbrush?

The word "puckerbrush" usually describes an area of land that is mostly composed of scrub-brush. Often land formerly used in farming, left neglected, becomes a thriving place for invasive species such as poison ivy, sumac, and buckthorn.

A second meaning of the word describes any incidence when a person is lost, or away from their normal understanding. It can describe a real, or imagined place. [For example, *"He is out in the puckerbrush."*]

> --- Janice A. Brown
> *New Hampshire Slanguage 2007*

Another insight comes from our friends north of the border in *Carleton County* (New Brunswick) *Colloquialisms.*

Word used to describe anywhere you didn't originally intend to be, a roadside ditch or stuck in the mud at the end of a disappearing trail *"He put his truck in the puckerbrush."* The term is likely derived from the common physiological reaction to finding oneself in the *puckerbrush.*

Most regions have their own synonym for Puckerbrush. I remember a sophisticated senior officer describing a small city in northern New York saying, "It's not the end of the Earth, but you can see it from there."

Here are some that the author has come across, think "Out in the _____"

- Boondocks, Boonies
- Outback
- Bush
- Backwoods
- Sticks
- Tules
- Hinterland
- In Back of Beyond
- Hollows
- Brambles
- Backwater
- Middle of Nowhere
- Willywags

For sophisticated Manhattanites: "with the bridge and tunnel people"

Please send me others at
puckerbrushnames@gmail.com